THE GHOST OF SLAPPY

R.L. STINE

SCHOLASTIC

THE GHOST OF SLAPPY

Goosebumps® MOST WANTED™

Scholastic Children's Books
An imprint of Scholastic Ltd
Euston House, 24 Eversholt Street, London, NW1 1DB, UK
Registered office: Westfield Road, Southam, Warwickshire, CV47 0RA
SCHOLASTIC, GOOSEBUMPS, GOOSEBUMPS HORRORLAND
and associated logos are trademarks and/or registered trademarks of Scholastic
Inc.

First Published in the US by Scholastic Inc, 2018
First published in the UK by Scholastic Ltd, 2019

Copyright © Scholastic Inc, 2018

ISBN 978 1407 19586 5

Goosebumps books created by Parachute Press, Inc.

A CIP catalogue record for this book
is available from the British Library.

Printed by CPI Group (UK) Ltd, Croydon, CR0 4YY
Papers used by Scholastic Children's Books are made
from wood grown in sustainable forests.

3 5 7 9 10 8 6 4 2

www.scholastic.co.uk

SLAPPY HERE, EVERYONE.

Welcome to My World.

Yes, it's *SlappyWorld*—you're only *screaming* in it! Hahaha.

Don't stare. I know you can't take your eyes off me. Most people wear sunglasses when they visit so they won't be *blinded* by my beauty! Hahaha!

I wish I had a phone so I could call myself and tell me how *awesome* I am! Hahaha.

I'm so cool, I give myself *goosebumps*. And then, guess what? I give my goosebumps *goosebumps*! Hahaha.

Did you see me on the cover of *DUMMY Magazine*? Of course you didn't! Don't call me Dummy, dummy!

I'm so smart, I can spell any word. I'm not kidding. I can spell any word. Want to see me do it? Okay. Here goes . . .

a-n-y-w-o-r-d

Hahahaha!

Well, I have a story to tell you—and you're lucky because it stars ME. Also, a kid named Shep Mooney. Shep is about to go on an overnight in the woods with his class.

I don't want to give anything away, but . . . it's probably going to be the scariest night of Shep's life. And *guess who* is going to make it scary? Hahahaha!

I call this one *The Ghost of Slappy.* Aren't you DYING to read it? Haha.

It's just one more terrifying tale from *SlappyWorld.*

1

I stuffed a pair of woolly socks into my duffel bag and frowned at my sister, Patti, who plopped on the edge of my bed. "Why are you staring at me? Why are you watching me pack?"

Her dark eyes flashed behind her glasses. "Because you're a hoot, Shep."

"Huh? I'm a hoot? What is a hoot? What are you talking about?"

She crawled over and began pawing through the bag. "Did you just pack a bar of soap?"

I slapped her hands away. "Get your paws off my stuff, Patti."

She stuck her round face into mine. "Did you? Did you just pack a bar of soap?"

"So what?" I said.

"It's an overnight in the woods, Shep. No one is going to take a shower."

I could feel my face grow a little hot. "Are you going to give me a break? I like to be prepared."

3

Truth is, I didn't really know *what* to pack. I'd never been on an overnight in the woods. I hate the woods. I hate the outdoors. And I'm not too crazy about the dark.

Why couldn't our sixth-grade class go on an overnight during the *day*?

Patti didn't back away. She sat beside my duffel bag with her arms crossed in front of her. I knew she was waiting to give me a hard time about something else.

Patti can be a pain. She is nine, three years younger than me. But she thinks she's the sensible one. Can she be bossy? Three guesses.

She has stringy black hair that she hates, a face as round as a pumpkin, and she has to wear glasses all the time. So do I. So do Mom and Dad.

Mom says it makes us look smart. But I think we look like a family of owls.

I tossed a flashlight into the bag. Patti pushed it deeper into the pile of stuff. "Could you go away?" I asked.

"Where should I go?"

"Brazil?" I continued to pack the duffel.

"You're a hoot, Shep," she repeated. "What did you just put in the bag? Was that bug spray?"

"Maybe," I said.

"It's almost November!" she shouted. "It's cold out. You're not going to need bug spray."

I pulled the can of bug spray out and tossed it on the bed. Sometimes Patti can be right.

4

Okay. So I was stressed. I wanted to bring all my blankets and my two soft pillows. I wanted to bring my sweaters and my sweatshirts in case it got really cold. But that seemed like too much.

Actually, I didn't want to bring anything. I didn't want to go. I kept thinking about being there in the dark with the trees rattling and shaking, and the wind howling, and all the wild animals lurking around everywhere.

And I knew I could not count on our teacher, Mr. Hanson, to help us feel safe. Hanson is a horror freak. Some kids call him Horrible Hanson because he loves everything that's horrible.

He tells us horror stories in class and talks about all the old movie monsters as if they were real. My friend Carlos Jackson and I know that he's been saving up ghost stories to tell on the overnight. There's nothing Horrible Hanson would like better than making us all scream our heads off in fright.

Carlos likes ghost stories. But I have a good reason for *hating* them, a reason I can't tell Carlos.

I jammed two wool ski caps into the bag. It was getting very full.

Patti laughed. "You've packed everything you own. Is Tootsie in there? You'd better let me look." Tootsie is our cat.

Patti jumped to her feet and searched through my stuff again.

"If you're so into it, why don't you go in my place?" I said.

She shook her head. "I can't go on a sixth-grade trip. I can only go with the cool kids."

"Huh? Fourth-grade kids are cool? Are you *kidding* me? You only learned to tie your shoes last week!"

She stuck her chin out. "We don't tie our shoes. We're too cool to tie our shoes."

I stopped and took a step back. I didn't want this to turn into a fight. I needed Patti's help.

I pushed my glasses up on my nose. "Would you do me a favor?"

"I don't think so," she said. "What is it?"

"My sleeping bag is in the basement. Could you bring it up for me?"

She squinted at me. "No way."

"But, Patti—"

"Shep, you have to get over this basement thing," she said. "You have *got* to stop being afraid of the basement."

"I—I can't," I stammered. "I told you. That's where I always run into Annalee."

She tossed back her head. "Annalee. How did you ever make up a name like Annalee?"

I couldn't help myself. I started to shout. "I didn't make it up! It's real. Her name is Annalee."

She gave me a shove. "Oh, please. Give it a rest. Like I'm really going to believe that stupid ghost story." She raised her hands to shove me again, but I backed out of her reach.

"Annalee—" I started.

"There's no Annalee," Patti said. "There's no ghost named Annalee haunting our house—and you know it. Why do you keep insisting?"

"Because it's true?" I said.

Patti rolled her eyes. "You're losing it."

"I don't know why she's haunting our house," I said. "And I don't know what she wants. B-but I know she's real. I saw her the day we moved in. And I've seen her again and again. And I have nightmares all the time about her."

"You dreamed her in a nightmare," Patti said. "She's not real."

"YES, SHE IS!" I screamed.

"Look at you. You're shaking," Patti said. She narrowed her eyes at me through her glasses. "You have *seriously* got to stop making up ghost stories. Ghosts do not exist, Shep. Everyone knows that ghosts don't exist."

I swallowed. "So you won't go down to the basement for me?"

She laughed. "You're a hoot."

I stopped at the top of the basement stairs. I peered down into the darkness. It smelled damp down there. It always smelled damp and kind of sour, like old newspapers or those dirty T-shirts that have been left on the floor in the back of my closet for a year or two.

I turned toward the kitchen. "Mom? Dad? Are you here? Can anyone go down to the basement for me?"

"Busy," I heard Mom call.

No answer from Dad.

I took a deep breath and reached to my neck for my lucky silver charm. Everyone should have a lucky silver charm. It has helped protect me in a lot of tough times.

It's actually a small silver bear head on a slender chain. You know. Like a charm on a charm bracelet. My grandfather Simon put it around my neck.

"Shepard, this is my lucky charm," he said. He was the only person in the world to call me by my full name. "I am giving it to you because my days are short and yours are long."

The cool silver tickled my skin.

"This lucky charm will never fail to bring you luck," Grandpa Simon said. "It has never failed me. You only need to press it between your fingers. Hold it tight and its luck will flow from the silver bear head to you."

I thanked him and adjusted the silver charm over my chest. Grandpa Simon died two weeks later. I've worn the lucky silver charm every day. I've never taken it off.

Now, I rubbed my fingers over it as I made my way down the basement steps. The stairs are wooden and steep, and they creak and groan like stairs in a horror movie.

As I neared the bottom, the stale aroma grew stronger. I heard the loud hum of the furnace against the back wall. I fumbled for the light switch.

Dim yellow light splashed over the basement. Two of the ceiling bulbs were out. But the one working bulb gave enough light to see the shelves against the far wall.

I knew my sleeping bag was rolled up on one of the shelves, next to my parents' skiing equipment and camping gear.

9

Holding my breath, I started to cross the basement. My sneakers thudded on the concrete floor. Dad was always talking about finishing the basement. Making it look nice. Turning it into a game room.

But somehow he never found the time to get it done. It still looked like a dark, damp, creep-out-time basement.

I kept my eyes straight ahead. I could see my sleeping bag tucked into a middle shelf. I was only a few feet away when a flash of light caught my eye and made me stop.

The light started out as a soft glimmer against the wall. Then it flickered like a tall candle flame and grew brighter. And as it did, I could see a figure forming in the center of the glow.

"Nooo . . ." A moan escaped my throat. "Annalee!"

She shimmered inside the flickering light. Just an outline of color. But then the outline filled in, and she stepped out of the white glow. A girl about my age. A girl in an old-fashioned, dark plaid skirt that brushed the floor. A high-collared white blouse with sleeves that billowed as if blown by the wind.

Her copper-colored hair fell below her shoulders and caught the glow of the light. Her eyes were large and blue and locked on me. She didn't blink. Her face . . . it was as pale as the light that surrounded her.

Hands reaching out to me, she appeared to float over the floor. The hem of her skirt made no sound as it brushed against the concrete.

As she loomed closer, I took a step back. And cleared my throat to shout: "Go away, Annalee!" My voice trembling and shrill, ringing off the low basement ceiling and the heavy walls.

"Go away, Annalee! You don't exist!"

A strange smile spread over her pale face. Too sad to be a smile. Her red hair fluttered around her shoulders. Her eyes stayed locked on mine.

My hand fumbled for the silver bear charm under my shirt. I grabbed it and squeezed it. "G-go away!" I stammered.

But she slid forward silently.

"What do you *want*?" I didn't recognize my shrill voice. "Annalee—what do you *want*?"

Her lips moved. Her words were lost, just a whisper of air.

She raised a pale, slender hand. Reached out— *to grab me?*

"Noooo!" I uttered a frightened cry—and toppled backward. I fell over a low pile of cardboard boxes. The boxes crashed to the floor. I thrashed the air with both hands as if grabbing for the ceiling.

But I fell hard. Thudded onto my back on top of a hard box.

"OOOOF." The air whooshed out of my chest. I struggled to catch my breath.

Annalee floated over me. Her hair flew around her face. Her lips moved again. Again, I couldn't hear what she was saying.

Her hands were curled into tight fists. She waved them at me.

Threatening me?

My heart pounded so hard, my chest ached. I couldn't think straight.

And then a voice from across the basement broke through my panic: "What *was* that? Shep? What fell?"

My mom, shouting from upstairs.

I squirmed and twisted, struggling to climb back onto my feet.

Mom's running footsteps thundered on the wooden basement stairs.

And before I could stand up, she was there. Leaning over me. Hands pressed to her waist. Her expression startled and confused.

"What on earth—"

I forced myself to sit up. "I—I—I—" I sputtered.

"Did you fall?" Mom asked.

"It was the GHOST!" I cried.

Where was she? I glanced around the basement, but I didn't see her.

"The ghost, Mom. Really. I—"

13

Mom offered me a hand and helped pull me to my feet.

"Annalee. She's here, Mom," I cried. "She's here."

Mom's mouth dropped open. She started to say something to me—but stopped. I realized she wasn't looking at me. Mom was squinting into the darkness.

"Oh, wow," Mom murmured. "I see her."

I gasped.

Mom took a few steps toward the center of the room. "There you are," she said, pointing. "I see you. You *do* exist, after all, don't you. Come into the light, Annalee. Do you want to come upstairs?"

4

I'm not stupid. It didn't take me long to realize that Mom was joking. That's what my parents both do when I tell them our house is haunted. They both make jokes.

I'm scared a lot of the time because of Annalee. I have nightmares. And I never want to be in the dark.

And their way of dealing with it is to make jokes and to tell me to "get over yourself."

One night, I heard my parents saying it's just a "phase" I'm going through—whatever that means. I guess they think I'll outgrow the whole thing.

Meanwhile, there's a ghost in the house. And the ghost wants something. I don't have a clue what it is. But she's always coming after me . . . Always reaching for me . . . Always trying to frighten me.

I grabbed my sleeping bag and followed Mom to the stairs. She rested a hand on my shoulder. "Did you hurt yourself when you fell?"

I shook my head. "I'm okay."

"You know, knocking over some cartons is no big deal," she said. "You don't have to make up a ghost story to explain it."

I stared hard at her. I wanted to scream that I didn't make it up. I wanted to scream that she should believe me. But I held myself back.

"Maybe someday you'll see her too," I muttered.

Mom didn't reply. We started up the stairs.

Patti stuck her head into the stairwell. "Shep, hurry," she shouted. "The bus is here."

"Huh?" I gasped. "I have more to pack. I need another sweater. I need my gloves."

Patti raised my duffel bag in front of her. "You packed your whole room. Mom, I think he packed his desk lamp."

"I did not!" I screamed.

Mom and Patti laughed. Mom thinks Patti is a riot.

I pulled my hoodie from the closet and tugged it on. Patti slapped the duffel bag into my chest. I grabbed it and the sleeping bag. Mom kissed my forehead and gave me a shove toward the front door. "Have fun!"

I opened the front door. The yellow school bus was parked at the curb. I could see there were a lot of kids already on it. I started down the front lawn.

"Look out! The ghost is following you!" Patti shouted.

16

I spun around. "How funny are you?" I asked sarcastically.

Patti laughed and pushed the front door shut.

I carried my duffel and sleeping bag to the bus. The luggage compartment was open. I slid my stuff inside.

Then I climbed the three steps onto the bus. I saw my best friend, Carlos, a few seats back. And I saw Mr. Hanson walking up the aisle. He waved to me.

The bus door closed. I turned and noticed the driver.

And jumped back with a cry.

The driver was slouched in the low leather seat. Both hands were on the wheel. He faced straight ahead, a broad grin frozen on his face.

The driver was some kind of big doll. A ventriloquist dummy!

5

Mr. Hanson laughed.

I turned and saw that he had his phone raised. Did he just snap my picture?

"That was sweet," he said. He tucked the phone into his jeans pocket. "You are the first one to actually jump, Shep. You almost fell off the bus!"

He laughed again and so did a lot of the kids. I didn't think it was that funny.

Hanson lifted the dummy out of the driver's seat. He waved to a white-haired woman in a blue uniform who was seated near the back of the bus. She came striding forward. I guessed she was the real driver.

The dummy's hard wooden head bumped me as Hanson carried it away. The dummy's eyes were green and glassy, and its painted, red-lipped grin was crooked. Something about it gave me the creeps.

18

"Take a seat," Hanson instructed me. "We'll see how Courtney Levitt reacts to our guest driver. Her house is next."

I dropped down next to Carlos. He had a bag of Twizzlers in his lap, and he offered me one. Before I could slide it from the bag, I felt a hard slap on the back of my head.

"Owww!"

I spun around—and stared at the grinning face of Trevor Pincus. My enemy.

Yes. I have an enemy.

Most kids don't have an enemy. But Trevor is mine. How did I get an enemy? Just lucky, I guess.

Actually, Trevor and I had been good friends. We hung out together. And we spent a lot of hours playing Xbox games at his house. We were good buddies. Until I kicked him during a school soccer game and broke his ankle.

Of course, it was an accident. I'd slipped on the grass and my feet slid out from under me.

I heard the horrible *craaack* from Trevor's ankle before I hit the ground. He just stood there staring wide-eyed, his mouth hanging open. Until the pain made him scream and he fell to his knees.

He had to have a few operations. And he walked on crutches for months.

How many times did I apologize? Maybe a thousand? My parents sent Trevor gifts. I hurried to his house as soon as he came out of the hospital to apologize some more times. But he refused to see me. Later, he wouldn't even talk to me or text me back ever.

So that was the end of our friendship. And the beginning of our enemyship.

And now from the bus seat behind me, Trevor gave the back of my head a hard slap. And he said, "You're such a total jerk, Shep. You screamed like a baby when you saw that stupid dummy in the driver's seat."

"Did not," I said through gritted teeth.

"Leave Shep alone," Carlos told Trevor.

"Who's going to make me?" Trevor kicked the back of my seat, so hard it made me snap forward, then back.

"Just ignore him," Carlos said to me. He handed me a Twizzler. We sat chewing. Trevor settled back in his seat.

Carlos eats only candy. I've never seen him eat much real food. He is big and tall and strong. So I guess it agrees with him.

Carlos is a good friend to have. For one thing, his parents work at the Springdale Riding Academy. So some weekends, Carlos and I get to feed the horses and hang out with them.

The bus slowed down and edged to the curb in front of Courtney Levitt's house. I've been to Courtney's house. Her family has a swimming pool in back. And one summer, Courtney invited me to one of her pool parties.

The driver opened the bus door. Then she climbed up and scurried to the back. Hanson quickly lowered the dummy into the driver's seat. He raised the dummy's hands to the steering wheel.

"Horrible Hanson strikes again," Carlos murmured. He offered me another Twizzler. "He gets such a charge out of scaring us."

"He's a menace," I whispered. "He wants us to live in a horror movie."

Carlos nodded. "I'll bet he's been saving his best ghost stories for the campfire tonight."

That sent a chill to the back of my neck. It made me think of Annalee. A picture flashed into my mind. The picture of her coming at me, that stern look on her face . . . reaching for me . . . reaching for me.

I shuddered.

"What's wrong?" Carlos asked, bumping my shoulder with his.

"Nothing," I said. I pointed out the window. "Here comes Courtney."

Courtney and her parents were striding down their driveway, carrying her overnight bag and backpack and sleeping bag.

Everyone got quiet. They all wanted to see how Courtney would react when she saw the dummy in the driver's seat. Hanson had his phone ready to snap her photo. He couldn't hide his excitement. He was actually giggling.

I leaned forward, my hands on the seat back in front of me. I watched Courtney climb onto the bus. She turned and gazed down the long aisle. I guessed she was trying to see who was already on board.

Then she turned to the driver. She squinted at the dummy for a moment. Then she grabbed its hand and shook it. "Nice to meet you. I'm Courtney," she said.

Everyone laughed. Hanson groaned. He lowered his phone. I could see how disappointed he was that Courtney didn't scream or act horrified.

"Take a seat, Courtney," he said. "Dawn Meadows's house is the next stop."

Courtney pushed past him, waving at some of her friends near the back.

Hanson reached for the dummy.

But he stopped when the bus door slammed shut. I heard a loud roar. Hanson's eyes bulged as the bus jerked forward. Hard.

The teacher stumbled and fell onto the front row. Sprawled over two kids.

Another roar. The bus lurched away from the curb.

Kids started to scream. Hanson struggled to stand up.

The bus rocketed down the middle of the street, picking up speed.

We were zigzagging crazily from side to side. The tires squealing. Engine thundering.

We were roaring away—*and the dummy was driving!*

Carlos and I were both screaming, gripping the seat backs in front of us. The bag of Twizzlers went flying into the aisle.

All around, kids were screaming and shouting, "Stop! Stop!"

Hanson struggled to his feet. His eyes still bulged and his face was as red as a tomato. He gripped the pole behind the driver's seat as the bus swung hard from left to right.

More screams as our bus scraped a parked car on the side of the street. The squeal of metal on metal rang in my ears.

Hanson came up behind the driver's seat. He reached out both hands to grab the dummy.

"Nooooooo."

A horrified moan escaped my throat as the dummy tossed back its head. I could see it clearly. I wasn't imagining it. The dummy had both hands on the wheel. And it tossed back its head and laughed—a shrill, evil laugh. The laugh sent chill after chill down my body, and I could feel the hairs rise on the back of my neck.

The white-haired driver staggered past, bumping the seats as she hurtled to the front. She squeezed past Hanson, bent forward, and grabbed the dummy around the waist with both hands.

The dummy continued its ugly laugh as the woman swept it up and heaved it at Hanson. Then she dived into the driver's seat and slowed the bus to a stop.

Hanson caught the dummy and held it tightly in front of him. The dummy kicked and thrashed and beat its head against Hanson's chest.

"I'm so sorry. I'm so sorry about this!" Hanson kept screaming to us.

A hush fell over the bus as Hanson fought to gain control over the squirming, twisting creature.

"I . . . don't . . . believe it," Carlos muttered. "This has to be one of Hanson's tricks, right?"

I opened my mouth to reply, but no sound came out.

It wasn't a trick. It couldn't be a trick.

But then . . . *what had we just seen?*

Hanson suddenly had a folded-up sheet of paper in his hand. I think he'd pulled it from the dummy's jacket pocket.

As the dummy struggled and squirmed, Hanson unfolded the paper in one hand. He raised it to his face and began to read in a desperate shout:

"Karru Marri Odonna Loma Molonu Karrano!"

The dummy stopped struggling. Its big, glassy eyes slid shut. Its wooden head lowered. And then its whole body slumped in Hanson's arms.

The teacher's mouth hung open. He was shaking. He squeezed the dummy tightly against him. He was wheezing with each breath.

Finally, he took a deep breath and held it. It seemed to calm him. He squeezed the dummy against his chest.

"I . . . I think we're safe now," Hanson said. "I put him to sleep. He isn't a danger anymore."

Then he cried out as the dummy slid from his arms and dropped to the floor.

Screams rang out all around. Carlos and I jumped to our feet.

The dummy crumpled in a heap in the aisle.

"Don't panic!" Hanson shouted. "Not a problem. I just dropped him."

He bent, wrapped one hand around the dummy's head, and lifted it off the floor. "He's harmless now," Hanson said. He waved for everyone to sit back down. "It's okay. He won't bother us again. He's not alive."

"You mean he *was* alive?" Carlos cried.

Hanson sighed. "It's a long story. I'll tell you the whole thing at the campfire tonight. But I swear this wasn't one of my tricks to scare you." He raised the dummy high. "This dummy is *way* too scary for me. I promise that he'll never come to life again."

If only our teacher had kept that promise . . .

SLAPPY HERE, EVERYONE.

Don't go away, folks. This story is just getting good.

You don't think I'd let a few magic words keep me from having fun—do you?

And for me, having fun is making sure *no one else does*!

Hahahahaha.

Aren't I a scream?

We hiked through the woods for most of the afternoon. We carried our bags and equipment with us. Mr. Hanson led us along a winding path, and we crunched through a thick blanket of dry brown leaves.

It was a cool October day. The sun floated very low over the bare tree branches, and the wind was gusty and strong.

We saw a family of rabbits and some brave squirrels that tried to stare us down. Mr. Hanson pointed to a bird high in the sky and said it was a hawk. But it was too small and plump to be a hawk. I'm pretty sure it was a pigeon.

Everyone was quiet the whole hike. I think we were all freaked by what had happened on the bus. I know I couldn't stop thinking about it.

Hanson had stuffed the dummy into his big duffel bag. I watched the bag bounce on his back as we walked. And I couldn't stop hearing the dummy's ugly laugh, again and again. His shrill, evil laugh as he crashed the bus down the street.

Hanson swore it wasn't a trick. But what else could it have been? Dummies don't come to life, do they? Only in the movies . . .

I was glad to arrive at the clearing where we were going to light the campfire, set up the tents, and spend the night. My back hurt from carrying all the equipment, and my stomach was growling. Carlos had a big bag of Peanut M&M's, which helped us get through the hike. But now I was hungry for dinner. Hungry and tired and drenched with sweat despite the cold evening air. I hate being outdoors. *Wish I were home having dinner*, I thought.

But then a picture of Annalee flashed into my mind. And I thought: *Maybe being out here with my friends is better than being home with a ghost.*

A circle of ashes and burnt wood chips in the center of the clearing showed where other groups had built their campfires. The sun had dropped below the trees, and the air was growing colder. We were going to need a big fire.

Hanson sent us all into the trees to gather firewood. Carlos and I worked together. There were sticks and tree branches all over the ground.

I held out my arms and Carlos piled wood on them. Soon I was carrying a tall stack, nearly as high as my head. "It's getting heavy," I groaned. "Let's go back."

I turned toward the clearing. But stopped when I heard a roar and the thunder of pounding feet over the leafy ground.

"Sneak attack!"

I heard the cry. Then I saw Trevor Pincus barreling toward us. He lowered his shoulder like a football running back—and rammed right into me with all his might.

"Ooof!" I uttered a choking cry. All the firewood went flying as I doubled over.

Trevor tossed back his head and laughed. "Sneak attack!" he repeated.

"Not funny." I burst forward, grabbed his shoulders, and gave him a shove.

He shoved back. "I thought it was hilarious!"

"Give us a break," Carlos yelled.

Trevor gave me another hard shove. "Can't take a joke?"

"*You're* a joke!" I said. I shoved him back.

Carlos moved to break up the shoving match. Trevor swept a pile of dead leaves into his hands and dropped them over Carlos's head. Then he laughed and took off, running back to the clearing.

"I hate having an enemy," I said. "I wish Trevor and I could get it together and make up."

"Make up? Yeah, sure. And I wish I had a Snickers bar as big as my head," Carlos said. "Know what I'm saying?"

By the time we got back to the clearing, everyone was setting up tents. The girls lined up their tents on the far side of the fire. The boys took the other side.

Carlos and I made sure our tent was far away from Trevor's. We didn't want any sneak attacks in the middle of the night.

Hanson made hot dogs on a charcoal grill for dinner. And we had potato salad and baked beans. I followed Carlos to the food table and grabbed a paper plate.

I stopped when I saw Maryjane Dewey smiling at me from across the table. I've had a crush on Maryjane ever since I was old enough to have crushes.

I think she's awesome. She has long black hair, which she keeps in a wide braid that goes down her back. Big green eyes. And a terrific smile. And she's funny and smart and very popular.

Maryjane seldom smiles at me, even though we sit next to each other in class. Truth is, she pretty much doesn't know I exist.

So you can imagine my shock when I saw the big smile she had for me at the food table. "Hi," I said. "How's it going?"

She didn't answer. Just kept smiling.

"Fun night, huh?" I said.

She blinked. "Oh. Shep. Hi."

"You . . . uh . . . were smiling at me, so I thought I'd say hi."

She laughed. "I was smiling at the hot dogs. I'm totally starving."

"Smiling at the hot dogs?"

She nodded.

Awkward.

I grabbed a couple of hot dogs, spun away from the table, and hurried to catch up to Carlos.

The sun had gone down. The sky was purple and filled with stars. I zipped my parka to the top and pulled the hood down over my head.

The fire crackled and blazed. The red and yellow flames swept high, reaching for the sky.

We huddled in a circle around the fire. Our faces were red in the firelight, with shadows flickering over us.

"Listen up, everyone," Hanson said, warming his hands in front of the fire. "I was going to tell a ghost story. But I think we've had enough scares for one day."

I breathed a sigh of relief. I really didn't want to hear a scary ghost story. I have my own *real* ghost story at home.

"I'm going to tell you the truth about that dummy," Hanson said. "It's a crazy, insane, unbelievable story. But I know you'll believe me—because you were there. You saw it with your own eyes. The dummy can come to life."

The fire crackled loudly and some logs toppled down. A few kids jumped at the sound. No one spoke. No one said a word.

"The dummy has a name," Hanson continued. "The name is Slappy. He's very old. I don't know exactly how old. I found him in my grandfather's attic. I don't know how he got there."

He crossed his legs and rubbed his hands together, warming them. "I started to do research on Slappy. Do you believe the dummy has his own Wikipedia page?"

Carlos and I exchanged glances. Was Hanson doing his usual horror-story routine? He had sworn this wasn't a joke.

"This is what I learned," he continued, raising his voice over the crackle of the fire. "Slappy was made by some kind of sorcerer. The dummy has powers. Evil magic. I mean, it can come to life."

Some kids started to murmur and whisper. Hanson waited for them to get silent again.

"There is a set of words. The words you heard me say on the bus. If you say the words aloud, Slappy will come to life. The only way to put him back to sleep is to say the words again."

"Are you making this all up?" Courtney Levitt demanded.

Hanson shook his head. "You *saw* it, Courtney. You saw me use the words to put Slappy back to sleep on the bus. This isn't a story. It's *real!*"

"And he's asleep now?" I asked. "He can't wake up?"

Hanson nodded. "He can't wake up on his own. Someone has to read the words to wake him up. And believe me, people—*no way* I'll ever say those words again!"

34

"He's, like, dead?" a boy on the other side of the fire demanded. "It's really safe to have him here?"

"He's like dead," Hanson said. "I made a terrible mistake. Last night—I said the words out loud. I didn't believe the whole story. I thought it was a joke. I said the words and . . . and you saw what happened on the bus this morning."

A lot of whispering and low voices around the fire. Then Trevor said, "If it's totally safe, can we see him again?"

That made a lot of kids chime in. Both yes and no.

"Do you really want to see him?" Hanson asked. "It's perfectly safe. Trust me. We can even pass him around."

More murmured conversations.

"Okay. Let's go get him," Hanson said. "You can see this evil guy close up." He pointed at Trevor. "The dummy is in my tent. Right over there. In the big duffel bag. Pull him out and bring him here, okay?"

Trevor gave Hanson a two-fingered salute. Then he climbed to his feet and took off, running to Hanson's tent. He disappeared into the tent. We all turned to watch.

The fire danced in front of us. I heard the *whoo whoo* of owls far away in the trees. I shivered and pulled my hoodie tighter around my face.

We watched Hanson's tent. And waited. It seemed to be taking Trevor a long time.

Hanson scratched his head. "I told him the big duffel bag. There's only one duffel bag," he said.

And then we all saw Trevor's head poke out of the tent. Trevor took a few steps toward us. "Mr. Hanson—" he called. "Mr. Hanson . . . the dummy—it's GONE!"

8

I gasped. A few kids uttered cries.

Hanson jumped to his feet. "That's impossible," he said. He spun away from the fire and began striding fast toward Trevor, swinging his fists at his sides. "You looked in the wrong place."

We watched Trevor follow Hanson into the tent.

"The dummy is still alive," I heard Dawn Meadows say. "He's out there somewhere." She jumped up. So did a bunch of other kids. They all turned slowly, peering into the dark trees.

"Hanson put him to sleep," someone said. "Trevor is just an idiot. He can never find anything."

"But what if the dummy came to life again? What then?"

"He's dangerous. He tried to *kill* us driving that bus."

"Did he run off? Is he in the woods? Waiting for us to go to sleep?"

37

"I'll never be able to sleep. We've got to get out of here."

"He's just a dummy. What can he do to us?" Carlos said to me.

"Hanson said he has evil powers," I said. "He . . . he could turn us all into wooden dummies!"

Carlos laughed. "You've seen too many horror movies."

"It isn't funny," I insisted. "If there's an evil dummy on the loose somewhere out there, we're definitely not safe." A shiver shook my whole body. I was scaring myself with my own words.

We all got silent as Hanson came bursting from the tent. Even from a distance, I could see the wild look on his face. He swept a hand tensely back over his hair. He spun slowly, peering into the trees all around.

"Slappy!" Hanson shouted at the top of his lungs. "Slappy! Are you out there?" His voice echoed off the trees.

No reply.

"Slappy—I know you're out there!" The teacher was trying to sound angry. But I could hear the fear in his voice. "Slappy—you can't get far! Come back here!"

Silence. The only sound was the crack and snap of the fire.

Hanson appeared to stagger as he walked

back to us. His eyes were wide, and he kept shaking his head.

I saw Trevor standing back by the tent. His hands were shoved deep in his coat pockets. He gazed into the trees, then slowly made his way back to the fire.

"Mr. Hanson, can we leave?" Maryjane asked. "Can we go home now? I . . . I don't feel safe."

A lot of others chimed in, all agreeing with Maryjane.

Hanson sighed. "We can't go home. The bus isn't coming to pick us up until tomorrow morning."

A lot of groans and moans. I squeezed my lucky silver charm tightly. I knew we all needed good luck.

Hanson shook his head again. "I just don't get it. I put him to sleep. You saw me. There's *no way* he could wake himself up."

"What can he do to us?" I blurted out. "Can he hurt us?"

"I don't know," Hanson replied, his face twisted in confusion. "I should have read more about him. I don't know *what* he can do."

He began pacing back and forth, taking long strides. He was muttering to himself, his lips moving. I couldn't hear what he was saying.

I turned to Carlos. "This is bad. Are you as scared as I am?"

He shrugged and kept his gaze on the fire.

"Mr. Hanson, can't we call for help?" Courtney asked.

Hanson stopped pacing. "I tried my phone. There are no cell towers out here. We can't make calls."

That got everyone moaning and murmuring.

I shivered again. I thought I saw something moving in the trees. But it was just low branches, shaking in the wind. "So what are we going to do?" I asked.

Hanson dropped back onto the ground. The fire had started to die. The flames were low and silent. "I'll keep guard all night," he said. "I'll stay awake. You will all be safe in your tents. If Slappy returns, I'll deal with him."

"You'll stay awake all night?" someone asked. "Are you sure—"

"I've done it lots of times," Hanson said. "It's not a problem. I'll stay alert." He thought for a moment. "But tell you what . . . If I feel myself getting drowsy, I'll wake up one of you. And we'll stand guard together."

It seemed like a plan.

So that's what we did. We helped build the fire high again. Then we left Hanson sitting there and hurried into our tents.

The ground was soft and damp now from the dew. And the air in the tent felt damp and nearly as cold as outside.

Carlos and I took off our coats but left our

clothes on. We burrowed deep into our sleeping bags. I tried to pull mine over my head. But I was too tall. I rested my head on my duffel bag.

"Think we can get to sleep?" I asked Carlos.

He didn't answer. I turned and saw that his eyes were closed and his mouth hung open. He was already asleep. Amazing.

I felt wide awake. My heart was pumping hard in my chest. I kept picturing the dummy . . . driving the bus . . . laughing that hideous laugh . . . kicking and squirming after Hanson picked him up.

I yawned. I was totally exhausted. But how could I stop thinking about the evil dummy? How could I ever get to sleep knowing that he was out there?

I was alert to every sound, every brush of wind, the creaking of the bare tree branches all around us, the crack of the fire.

I closed my eyes. I tried to shut my mind, push everything away, become a blank sheet of paper.

I guess I finally drifted off into a restless sleep. I was aware of trying to roll over inside the sleeping bag. I don't know how long I slept. But I awoke with a startled cry. It took a few seconds to remember where I was.

I rubbed my face. It felt cold and wet. I turned and saw that Carlos was still asleep.

Now fully awake, I slid out of the warmth of

the sleeping bag, into the cold air. I crawled to the tent flap and pushed it open. The sky was still black. I guessed I hadn't slept for long.

The fire was low. Just a few licks of purple flames.

I climbed to my feet and stepped out. I gasped when I saw Hanson sitting in front of the fire. He was lit by the dull flicker of the dying flames. His body was slumped and his head was down.

My heart pounding, I tugged on my sneakers. I didn't bother to tie them. I took off, running to Hanson. My shoes pounded the frosty ground. I stopped a few yards behind him. I could hear him snoring.

Hanson was sound asleep.

I stood and stared at him for a long moment. Then I peered into the woods. No sign of the evil dummy.

What should I do? My mind raced with ideas.

I was wide awake. I could stand guard till Hanson woke up.

A lot of kids called me a wimp because I hate being outdoors and I hate long hikes and overnights. This would prove to them that I'm a take-charge guy.

Maybe Maryjane Dewey would notice me.

I realized I was shaking. I needed my parka and hood. I spun around, my shoes slipping on the frosted ground. I began to run back to my tent.

I was just a few yards away when I heard the footsteps.

I stopped with a gasp. And listened.

A soft thump. Then another.

From behind my tent. Coming closer.

I held my breath. I stared into the darkness.

I couldn't see anything. But I heard them. I wasn't imagining it.

I heard the soft, steady thump of approaching footsteps.

I froze. I couldn't breathe. I couldn't move.

The dummy waited till the middle of the night to return, I thought.

NOW what does it plan to do?

I heard another soft *thump*. Closer.

I sucked in a deep breath. I turned back toward Hanson and opened my mouth to scream.

But only a choking cough escaped my throat.

With a shudder, I spun back. And saw it.

It stepped out from behind my tent.

The biggest rabbit I've ever seen.

Standing upright. Hopping on two legs. Its ears standing tall.

Thump thump.

"Oh, wow." I dropped to my knees. "Oh, wow. I'm an idiot."

The rabbit winked, as if agreeing with me.

"Everyone okay?" Hanson asked as we gathered the next morning. "No problems last night?"

No one had any problems.

Carlos yawned and stretched. "Did you sleep?" he asked me.

I shook my head. "Not much." *No way* I was going to tell him about my scary bunny incident. I knew he would laugh for half an hour.

"The dummy is probably miles from here by now," Hanson said. He scratched his head, which made his hair stand out in clumps. "But just in case . . . As you pack up, keep an eye out for him."

We had a fast breakfast of cold Corn Flakes and an energy bar. Carlos had a bag of candy corn, so we had that for dessert. Then we packed up our stuff as if we were all on fast-forward. I don't think anyone ever packed up a campsite faster.

We had a different bus driver on the way back. I told Carlos, "I'll bet that other driver was so freaked by the dummy, she ripped up her driver's license."

"She's not the only one who's freaked," Carlos said. "We all are."

He was right. The bus was nearly silent the whole way back to town. No one felt like talking. Hanson sat in the front seat with his head lowered, his face buried in his hands.

As we neared the first stop—Dawn's house—he stood up. He gazed down the long row of silent kids. "I'm totally puzzled," he said. "I don't know what to tell you. If you want to tell your parents what happened . . ."

45

He rubbed his face. ". . . It will cause a big fuss," he continued. "I know I'm going to be in a lot of trouble. And I guess I deserve it for bringing that dummy in the first place."

He paused for a moment. The bus lurched to a stop, and he nearly fell over.

"I want to warn you that your parents may not believe you," he continued. "I mean, who would believe it? But it's completely up to you if you want to tell your parents about Slappy or not."

He stood holding on to the pole. I could see that he was thinking hard. "I *do* know one thing for sure," he said finally. "That dummy is long gone. We will never see him again."

"How was it?" Mom asked. She greeted me at the door. She wanted to hug me, but I was lugging all my stuff.

I dragged my duffel and sleeping bag into the house and dropped them in the front entryway. Then I had my hug with Mom.

"Did you have fun?" Dad asked, walking into the living room from the kitchen. He was drying his hands on a dish towel.

Both of my parents work at home. So I always see both of them all the time.

"Fun? Not really," I said. "It was . . . weird."

"Weird? What do you mean weird?" Dad demanded.

"Were you cold all night?" Mom asked.

46

"Cold wasn't the problem," I said. "It's . . . kind of a long story."

You see, an evil ventriloquist dummy came to life, nearly crashed our school bus, then ran off into the woods.

If I said that, Mom and Dad would laugh. They'd think I was joking. They'd ask me what *really* happened.

I picked up the duffel and tucked the rolled-up sleeping bag under one arm. "Let me unpack," I told them. "Then I'll come down and tell you the whole story."

Yes, I was stalling for time.

But what would *you* do?

Mom followed me to the stairs. "Do you want help unpacking?"

"No. I can handle it," I said. "No problem. I'll be down in five minutes."

"I'm making tomato soup for lunch," Dad said. He's the cook in the family. "Do you want a sandwich with it?"

I shrugged. "Whatever. I'm not that hungry."

You see, I was up all night scared out of my mind. And it kind of took away my appetite.

I dragged my stuff up the stairs. My duffel felt as if it weighed a hundred pounds. Did I really pack so much for one night?

I stepped into my room, when I remembered that the sleeping bag went down in the basement. I decided to take it down later. I didn't want to think about the basement right now. I didn't want to think about the ghost waiting for me down there.

My brain was whirring about how to explain to my parents why the overnight was weird. *"You probably won't believe this, but . . ."*

I heaved the duffel bag onto my bed and unzipped it. I had emptied half of my dresser into it, and of course I didn't need any of the stuff I brought. I never changed my clothes.

I pulled out the pair of jeans I'd packed, two sweatshirts, two pairs of socks, a spare hoodie . . . I grabbed them from the duffel and tossed them in a pile on the bed.

Then I peered into the bag to see if I'd gotten everything. And I let out a cry. And froze . . .

As I stared at Slappy the dummy grinning up at me.

10

His eyes were locked in a glassy stare. His mouth gaped open in a frozen grin. The dummy was folded in half, its legs tucked beneath it.

My heart started to pound. I kept blinking, expecting it to vanish, just an example of my imagination gone berserk.

But no. The dummy was tucked into the bottom of my duffel. I took a deep breath and lifted it out.

My whole body was tense. I expected Slappy to kick or twist or swing his arms. But the arms and legs dangled limply at his sides. The eyes closed as I raised him in front of me. His mouth hung open lifelessly.

"You're not awake," I said out loud. "Tell me. You're not awake—right?" I shook it. Shook it hard.

The head bounced back. The arms and legs hung loosely.

"Are you pretending to be asleep?" I demanded. I shook the dummy as hard as I could.

And a folded-up sheet of yellow paper fell from inside its jacket and fluttered to the floor.

"Whoa." I lowered the dummy to the bed. Then bent to pick up the piece of paper. My hands trembled as I unfolded it. Was this the secret words to bring Slappy to life?

No.

It was a message. Written in red marker:

HERE'S YOUR NEW BEST FRIEND. HAVE FUN WITH HIM.

I didn't have to guess about who wrote the note. And gazing at it, reading it a second and third time, I knew who had tucked the dummy into the bottom of my duffel.

Trevor Pincus.

My enemy.

I knew his handwriting. This wasn't the first note I ever got from Trevor. But so far it was the most frightening.

Last night, Hanson sent Trevor to his tent to get Slappy. Now I knew what took him so long. Trevor took the dummy from Hanson's tent and stuffed it into my bag. Then he came out and yelled to everyone, "IT'S GONE!"

Just the kind of mean trick an enemy would pull.

I crumpled the note and tossed it to the floor. I turned back to the dummy. "Are you pretending to be asleep? Are you saving your evil plans for later?"

I knew I couldn't keep it here. Trevor knew I'd

be terrified to have it in my house. And who wouldn't be?

I had to get rid of it. Maybe sneak it into Trevor's house? No. That would just start a dummy-trading war. I needed to get it out of the house for good.

Return it to Hanson?

That seemed like a plan. But I didn't want Hanson to think I stole it.

I stood there gaping at the dummy in my bed. Mom's voice floated up from downstairs. "Shep? What's taking so long? Lunchtime. Soup's on."

"I . . . I'll be down in two minutes," I called.

I grabbed the dummy off the bed, darted across my room, and heaved it to the back of my clothes closet. I slammed the closet door shut.

"Well, hurry up," she called. "Your soup is getting cold."

Cold soup wasn't my biggest problem. I kept my eyes on the closet door. I pictured it bursting open and the dummy leaping out to attack me.

I fumbled my phone out of my pocket. Almost out of power. I texted Carlos: ARE YOU THERE? NEED YOU TO COME OVER. FAST.

Carlos was a lot calmer than me. He'd help me figure out how to return it to Hanson without getting into trouble.

The phone trembled in my hand. I kept glancing at the closet door, then staring at the phone. "Carlos—where are you?"

"Shep! Come downstairs—now!" Mom shouted from downstairs.

"Coming! Be right there!" I called.

My phone made a *ding* sound. A text popped up on my screen. I squinted at it—and gasped.

I'M READY TO PLAY, SHEP. ARE YOU READY TO PLAY? Slappy

11

I swallowed hard. *This can't be happening.*

It took me a few seconds to get it together and realize that Slappy the dummy hadn't texted me from the closet.

Trevor had sent the text.

What a fun guy.

I let out an angry cry and started to text him back. But I stopped after the first sentence.

"I'm not going to answer. I'm going to ignore you, Trevor," I said out loud. "I'm not going to play your game."

I started to click off the message screen. But the phone chimed again and another text appeared. This one from Carlos: CAN'T COME TILL AFTER DINNER

I sighed, disappointed. I wanted to get rid of Slappy immediately. But I figured I could wait till later. I took one more hard look at the closet door. All was still and quiet. So I hurried downstairs for my tomato soup.

"Well, tell us about the overnight," Mom said as I took my place at the table. "What was so weird about it?"

"Well . . . to begin with, we had bus trouble," I said. "I think the driver was crazy or something. We almost crashed a few times."

I'd decided not to tell them about Slappy. Mr. Hanson was probably right. They wouldn't believe me anyway. Plus, they never believed my stories about Annalee. Our house is totally *haunted*, and they refuse to even think about it. So they would never believe this. Anyway, I planned to have Slappy out of the house and gone forever that night. So they never needed to know about him.

The soup was good. I told them a few things about the overnight. Told them about the big rabbit that almost invaded our tent. Nothing too interesting.

After lunch, you can imagine how long the afternoon felt. I tried to read some of my English assignment, but the text was just a blur. And the algebra worksheet looked like a bunch of strange numbers and letters to me.

I just couldn't think straight. I stayed in my room because I wanted to keep guard over the closet. But I probably should have gotten out of there so that I could clear my mind.

When Patti came home, she wanted to play this bubble-bursting video game that she loves.

So I played with her for a while. I thought it might take my mind off the dummy in the closet. But Patti is too good at the game, and I ended up just watching her blast and burst all the bubbles. I hardly got a turn.

At dinner, Patti teased me about the overnight. "Did you see any ghosts, Shep? Was your tent haunted?"

"Yeah. Carlos and I stayed up all night, playing hide-n-seek in the woods with a bunch of ghosts," I said. "They were real good at hiding."

I was bursting to tell her the *real* story. But somehow I held it in.

I didn't feel like eating. My stomach felt like it was tied in a tight knot. I couldn't stop thinking about the dummy upstairs in my closet and how I had to get it out of the house. Somehow, I forced myself to eat half a plate of spaghetti.

After dinner, I went up to my room to wait for Carlos. I texted him. He said he was on the way.

Hurry! I typed.

What's the emergency? he texted back, but I didn't answer.

I definitely couldn't tell him over the phone. I was afraid he might not come.

I stood in the middle of my room with my arms crossed tightly in front of me. I tried to force away the chills that were running down my back.

"Carlos? Where *are* you?" I murmured.

55

I cried out when I heard a sound. From inside the closet?

I held my breath and listened.

Yes. A scraping sound. Definitely inside the closet.

And then a metallic sound, the clang of clothes hangers hitting each other.

"Ohhhhhh." I stared wide-eyed at the closet door, as if trying to see through the wood.

Another soft *clang*.

My whole body shuddered.

Without thinking, I moved to the closet. My hand felt icy cold against the metal doorknob.

With a hard tug, I pulled open the door—stared into a pulsing white light—and leaped back in horror as Annalee came bursting out, howling a shrill animal howl, reaching for me . . . reaching . . .

Her long red hair billowed over her head as she flew from the eerie light behind her. Her eyes were pale, so pale they appeared totally white. And her mouth was open in a silent screech.

What was she doing here? She had never come upstairs before.

I ducked as she grabbed at me. A gust of cold air followed her hand. The whole room had grown cold. I dropped to my knees as she came at me again.

The icy wind swirled around me. I raised my

eyes and saw her mouthing a word, over and over. Was it my name?

She floated lower. I tried to roll away.

I could see through her hands as she reached for me. I saw right through them as she came closer . . .

I couldn't keep it in any longer. I opened my mouth and screamed at the top of my lungs.

"Noooooooo! NOOOOOOOO!"

12

Somehow, I scrambled to my feet. Struggling to catch my breath, my heart thudding noisily in my chest, I lurched to the bedroom door—and out into the hall.

I stopped when I saw Carlos at the top of the stairs. He came rushing toward me. "What's wrong?" he cried. "Shep? What is it?"

"I . . . uh . . ." I struggled to choke out some words. "Inside . . ." I pointed frantically to my room.

Carlos brushed past me and stepped inside. I hesitated for a moment, then followed him in.

Carlos gazed all around.

There was nothing to see. The closet door was open. But there was no eerie, pulsing light. No Annalee. Nothing. Nothing at all.

He turned to me. "Why did you scream like that?"

Think fast, Shep.

"Oh. I . . . uh . . . I stubbed my toe," I said. I hopped on one leg, wrapping my hand around the other foot. "Wow. That was really *intense*. Hope I didn't break the toe."

He squinted at me. I'm not sure whether he believed me or not. Finally, he shrugged and dropped down on the edge of my bed.

"Don't sit down. We have work to do," I said.

"What are you talking about?" he demanded. "Didn't you call me over to play *World of War*? Where's your Xbox?"

"We don't have time for games," I said. "This is serious."

Carlos stared at me but didn't reply. He was waiting for me to explain.

Instead, I crossed to the closet. My heart skipped a beat. Was Annalee waiting inside to ambush me?

Heart pounding, I ducked my head in and peered all around. Dark now. No pulsing light. Slappy was sprawled on the floor where I'd left him, eyes shut, mouth hanging open.

I lifted the dummy off the closet floor and carried him out.

"Whoa!" Carlos let out a startled cry and jumped to his feet. "How did you get that? Is he alive?"

I shook my head. "He's asleep. I made sure."

Carlos took a few steps toward me, eyes on the dummy. "You're sure?"

I nodded.

"He—he didn't just show up here—did he?" Carlos stammered.

"No way," I said. "Trevor stuffed him in my duffel. A little surprise."

Carlos reached out and squeezed the sleeve of the dummy's jacket. "Trevor didn't make him come alive before he gave him to you?"

"No," I insisted. "I'm sure he's asleep. He's not dangerous."

"Did you tell your parents?"

I shook my head again. "I didn't want to. Did you tell *your* parents about him?"

"No," Carlos said. "They'd laugh and tell me I should be a sci-fi writer. They're always telling me what I should be."

"Want to hold him?" I asked.

Carlos shrugged. "Not really. What do you plan to do with this thing? You're not going to keep it, are you?"

"No way," I said. "It's evil. If it comes to life . . ."

Carlos squeezed one of the dummy's shoes. "So you're going to give it back to Hanson?"

"Tonight," I said. "That's why I needed your help. We have to figure out how to return it to Hanson. And we have to do it now. We have to get it out of this house. I'm totally creeped out, Carlos. I'll never sleep again if we don't—"

"But we don't know where Hanson lives," Carlos said. "I think someone told me he lives in Harris Falls. That's two towns from here."

I let out a sigh. "Oh, wow."

"Wait. Wait," Carlos said. His eyes were shut

in concentration. "We don't have to bring it to his house. We'll carry it to school and put it in Hanson's classroom. You know. Maybe sit it up in his desk chair."

"That's good," I said. "But it's night, Carlos. How do we get into the school?"

"There's bound to be a back door or a window open somewhere." He frowned. "But . . . if we get caught . . ."

"We'll be careful," I said. "We won't get caught. And if we do, we'll just say—"

I didn't get a chance to finish my sentence, because Patti came barging into my room. "Hey, Carlos!" she shouted. She slapped him a high five. Then she saw the dummy in my arms.

Patti laughed. "I don't believe it. You're playing with dolls now? Do you want to borrow my Bratz collection?"

"I'm not playing with dolls," I said. "It's a dummy, not a doll."

"That makes *two* dummies in here," she said. Then she laughed at her own lame joke.

"Why are you in my room?" I snapped. "Get out. Seriously. You weren't invited."

She reached for Slappy. "Let me hold him."

"No way, Patti. He doesn't belong to me. Get lost. I mean it."

"I just want to hold him," she insisted. She grabbed both of the dummy's legs and began to pull.

"Let go!" I shouted. "I said let go. You can't—"

61

She gave a hard tug and the dummy slid out of my grasp. Its head hit the carpet as Patti swung it away from me. And something fell out of its jacket pocket. A small piece of paper.

I grabbed for it. But Patti got there first.

She held the dummy under one arm and raised the paper to her face with her other hand.

"Hey, what does this mean?" she asked. "Karru Marri Odonna Loma Molonu Karrano."

13

I gasped and dropped back. Carlos started to choke.

I gaped at the dummy, waiting for it to start moving.

Patti laughed. "What's your problem?" She fluttered the paper in front of me. "Do you know what the words mean?"

I swiped the dummy from under Patti's arm. "You—you don't know what you just did," I stammered.

"You brought the dummy to life!" Carlos cried. "It's evil, Patti. It's an evil thing. And you just brought it to life!"

Patti narrowed her eyes at Carlos. "You're joking, right? You know, I'm nine years old. I'm not a baby. If you're trying to scare me . . ."

"We're *both* scared," I said. "We've seen it come alive. We've seen it—"

Patti laughed. "You're both pitiful. Seriously. You're not funny." She started from the room, but turned back at the doorway. "Hey, I've got an awesome idea, Shep. Why not introduce the living dummy to your ghost friend? You can all have a party!" She disappeared down the hall, laughing as if she'd just had a great triumph.

I held the dummy by the waist. A chill tightened the back of my neck. I raised Slappy and stared at his face. His eyes were as glassy and lifeless as always. His mouth hung open. Arms and legs dangled limply.

"Not alive," I said.

Carlos remained a few feet away. I saw drops of sweat rolling down his forehead. His face was knotted in concentration as he studied the dummy.

"But your dumb sister read the words," he said.

"He isn't moving or anything," I said. "Maybe he was alive when he arrived here. Maybe he was pretending to be asleep the whole time, and—"

"Maybe he's pretending to be asleep right now," Carlos said. "Maybe he's just waiting . . ."

"Waiting for what?"

"Waiting for the right time to do something horrible to us."

The dummy was getting heavy. I swung it over my shoulder. Its head bounced against my back.

"Let's not give it a chance," I said. "Hurry—let's carry him to school."

Carlos hesitated at the door. "Your parents—"

"They're in the den. Your job is to distract

them. Go talk to them while I sneak the dummy out the garage door."

Carlos eyed the dummy. "Okay. We can do this. I know we can."

"It's only four blocks," I said. I glanced out my window. The sky was dark purple and I saw big snowflakes drifting straight down. "Four blocks in the snow."

"We can do this," Carlos said again. He was giving himself a pep talk.

"Go talk to my parents," I said. "I only need two minutes to get my coat and sneak outside."

Carlos disappeared into the hall. I started after him. We both trotted down the stairs. Carlos turned toward the den in the back of the house.

I made my way to the coat closet in the front. I could hear the TV on in the den. Mom and Dad were talking over it. I heard them greet Carlos.

I pulled open the closet door. Then I swung the dummy off my shoulder so I could grab my coat.

I lowered Slappy in front of me. And as I lowered him, his wooden hand brushed my cheek. And then I felt something grab my nose. Something hard grabbed my nose and started to squeeze.

The dummy's hand. The wooden hand. The fingers had wrapped around my nose. And now the pain shot up my face. The fingers squeezed harder. My eyes began to tear. I shut them against the pain. My whole head throbbed.

I opened my mouth to scream. But only a squeak escaped my throat.

"L-let go!" I stammered in a whisper.

I had the dummy by the waist. I pulled . . . pulled hard. But that only made the pain grow sharper.

"You're breaking my nose!" I managed to choke out.

The fingers tightened and began to twist.

Was he trying to pull my nose off?

I shoved him away. Grabbed his arm. Tried to pry the fingers away from my face.

But he was too strong.

The pain throbbed everywhere. And I started to see red. And my knees started to fold. I was going down. Down into a rising darkness of pain.

14

Suddenly, the wooden fingers loosened their grip. The dummy's hand fell away. I stood gasping, wheezing, struggling to catch my breath.

The pain throbbed over my entire face. I tried to speak but only choking grunts escaped my throat. I staggered to the wall. Raised my hand gently to my nose.

"Owwww!"

I pulled my hand away. My nose was too tender to touch.

Then I saw Patti, standing a few feet away, studying me, her eyes narrowed behind her round glasses, hands on her waist. "Shep, have you totally lost it?" she demanded. "Why are you standing out here with that doll? Where did Carlos go?"

I managed to find my voice. "He's . . . in the den."

"Why do you have your coat? Where are you taking the doll?" Patti asked. But she didn't wait for an answer. She stepped up to me, her eyes on my nose. "Shep—what did you do to your nose?"

"Uh . . . bumped it," I said.

She reached up and squeezed it.

"YAAAAIIIIII." I let out a cry that could be heard for blocks. I dove back out of her reach.

"Bumped it on *what*?" she demanded. "You could play Rudolph the Reindeer in the Christmas pageant."

"Bumped it on . . . something," I muttered. I was in too much pain to think of a good lie.

"You should put ice on it," Patti said. "That's what Mom always says to do. Want me to get you an ice pack?"

"Uh . . . yeah. Sure. Thanks," I said. *Anything to get rid of her.*

She pushed past me and began hurrying to the kitchen. I waited till she was out of sight. Then I swung the dummy over my shoulder and crept to the side door that led to the garage.

I could hear Carlos still chatting with my parents in the den. I heard Patti open the freezer door in the kitchen.

I grabbed the doorknob. I could feel the tension rising in my throat, in my pulsing heartbeats. My whole body tingled with dread.

One more step. One step into the garage. And I'd be on my way. On my way to saying good-bye to this evil creature.

I reached under my coat and squeezed my silver bear charm for luck. Then I twisted the doorknob. Started to pull the door open.

And Slappy raised his head and screamed in a high, shrill voice: "HELP! I'M BEING KIDNAPPED! SOMEBODY—HELP ME!"

15

"Oh nooo." My whole body slumped. My hand fell away from the doorknob.

"HELP ME! PLEASE!" Slappy screeched.

I heard the thud of footsteps from the kitchen and den. Patti, Mom, Dad, and Carlos all came stampeding. I saw Mom and Dad's eyes bulge when they saw me at the side door. They stared at the dummy draped over my shoulder.

"What's *that*?" Mom cried.

"Shep, were you sneaking out?" Dad demanded.

"That's his new doll!" Patti exclaimed.

Carlos hung back. He just shook his head. He knew I was in trouble here.

I pressed my back against the door. The dummy didn't move. It hung limply over my shoulder.

"Did you make that funny voice?" Mom asked.

"Uh . . . yeah," I lied. My heart had leaped to my throat. My voice came out choked and dry. "I've . . . uh . . . been practicing in my room. Carlos saw me."

They turned to Carlos. He nodded.

"Where did you get that dummy?" Dad asked.

"Mr. Hanson let me borrow it," I said. One good lie deserves another. I swung the dummy around and held it by its head. "But I have to take it back to him."

"You weren't planning on doing that now—were you?" Dad demanded. "It's late."

"Well . . . no," I said. "I just brought it down to show it to you. I'll bring it back to Mr. Hanson tomorrow."

"I read some weird words on a piece of paper," Patti chimed in. "And they said I brought the doll to life."

Carlos and I laughed. "We were just joking."

"CUZ YOU'RE A BIG JOKE!" Slappy yelled.

"Oh . . . !" I gasped.

"Shep, stop that," Mom said. "That's not funny."

I covered the dummy's mouth, but he bit my finger. "MRS. MOONEY," he shrieked at my mom. "ARE THOSE ORANGE AND BROWN DESIGNS ON YOUR BLOUSE—OR DID YOU BURP UP YOUR DINNER?"

"Shep—I mean it," Mom said, narrowing her eyes at me and tightening her lips in her angry look. "Your jokes are mean. They're not funny."

"ARE YOU AN ACTRESS? YOU'VE GOT A GOOD FACE FOR HORROR MOVIES!" Slappy shouted at her.

I wrapped both hands around his mouth, trying to make him stop.

"Take it upstairs," Dad said. "We don't want
to hear any more."

Mom squinted at me, suspicious. "How did you
learn to throw your voice like that?"

"I . . . I didn't," I stammered. "It's the dummy.
The dummy is talking. Not me."

Mom rolled her eyes. "Very funny."

"I'm not kidding, Mom. I—"

"He's telling the truth," Carlos said. "The
dummy is alive. He's making the bad-news jokes."

Dad laughed. "You're a good friend, Carlos. But
you don't have to make up stories like Shep does."

"Well, take him to your room. Your jokes are
gross," Mom said.

"Can I have him?" Patti tried to grab him. I
swung him out of her reach.

"No way. He has to go back to Mr. Hanson
tomorrow."

"HANSON IS SO DUMB, HIS IQ IS THE
SAME AS HIS SHOE SIZE!" Slappy screamed.

Dad squeezed my shoulder and pointed to the
stairs. "Upstairs. Now. I mean it."

"Uh . . . maybe I'll just leave him in the garage,"
I said, turning and reaching for the door.

I didn't want the evil thing in my room all
night. I wouldn't get one second of sleep. There
is no lock on my closet door. No way I could be
safe from him.

"Look at Shep's nose," Patti said, pointing. "Doesn't it remind you of that cauliflower you bought at the supermarket, Mom?"

"It's okay," I said. "I bumped it, that's all. It doesn't hurt. Really."

"A CAULIFLOWER LOOKS GORGEOUS NEXT TO YOU!" Slappy screamed at Patti. "WHY DON'T YOU DO SOMETHING ABOUT THAT WART? OH, I'M SORRY. THAT'S YOUR FACE!"

"Mom, make him stop," Patti said. She gave me a hard shove. Slappy almost fell out of my hands.

"Your jokes are terrible!" Mom cried. "What's gotten into you, Shep? You've never acted like this before."

"Sorry," I murmured. I gave up. I knew I couldn't convince them that Slappy was talking on his own.

I pulled open the garage door. "Just putting the dummy out here until the morning."

I folded Slappy in half and shoved him on a shelf next to the charcoal and barbecue grill equipment. Then I hurried back into the house. I didn't feel much safer with Slappy in the garage. I knew what I had to do.

My parents had returned to the den. Carlos and Patti stood by the door. "You two, come upstairs with me," I said.

"I can't," Carlos replied. "I have to get home. My parents are texting me."

"But, Carlos—"

"Sorry," he said. He pulled his coat from the front closet. "Tomorrow, okay?"

"But the dummy—"

Carlos had strict parents. He tried hard not to get on their bad sides. Especially now. His birthday was coming up, and his parents had planned a spectacular party for him. It was going to be at the stables where they worked. And there was going to be horseback riding and everything.

Carlos didn't want to mess that up. He gave me a wave and headed out the front door.

I tugged Patti's arm. "Come up to my room. This is all your fault, anyway."

She pulled free. "My fault? Why are you acting so weird?"

I waited until we were in my room. I closed the door behind us. "I'm acting weird because you really *did* bring that dummy to life."

Patti laughed. "You don't give up, do you? Why are you trying to scare me?"

I balled my hands into tight fists. "It's not a joke. But you don't have to believe me. Just give me back that piece of paper with the secret words on them."

She blinked. "Huh? Piece of paper?"

"Don't act dumb. You took the piece of paper and you read the words. I need it back."

She took off her glasses and rubbed them on the sleeve of her T-shirt. "I *did* give it back to you."

"No, you didn't," I said. I gave her a push. "Go look in your room. Maybe you took it to your room."

"I don't think so," she said. "Did you look in here? Did you look on the floor? Under your bed?"

"I'll look and you look," I said. "But hurry. I need it right away."

"Why don't you make up your own magic words?" she asked.

I gave her another push. "Just go find it."

If I could read the words out loud, it would put Slappy back to sleep. And my worries would be over.

I searched frantically in my room. I crawled under my bed and under my desk. I searched in the closet. I even tore off the bedcovers and looked under them.

I was on my hands and knees, peering under the dresser, when Patti returned. "Did you find it?" I cried, my voice high and trembling. "Did you?"

She shook her head. "Not in my room."

"But, Patti—" I was so wired, I almost burst into tears.

"Maybe we tucked it back into the dummy's jacket pocket," she said. "Remember? It fell out of his jacket? Maybe we stuffed the paper back in after I read the words."

"Yes!" I cried, jumping to my feet.

That had to be it. That *had* to be the answer.

We tucked the sheet of paper back. Of course.

"Thanks," I said. I patted her on the head.

Then I ran out the bedroom door and down the stairs. Mom and Dad were still in the den. My heart started to pound real hard again as I stepped up to the door to the garage.

I pulled it open and lurched into the garage.

The first thing I saw was that the big sliding garage door was wide open.

The second thing I saw was that Slappy was gone.

SLAPPY HERE, EVERYONE.

"Karru Marri Odonna Loma Molonu Karrano."

I love those words. They always make me feel so ALIVE! Hahaha.

Those words are like a song to me. A song that makes me want to dance—on someone's face! HAHAHAHA.

I don't know *what* the words mean. They probably mean something like "Slappy is awesome."

Hahahaha.

I don't *care* what they mean. To me, they only mean one thing—it's *magic time*!

And my kind of magic is making people scream.

Are *you* ready for my next trick?

Hahahaha!

I stood there in the garage, stunned for a long moment. I stared at the snow falling in big flakes outside the open door. I listened to the swirl of wind coming around the side of the garage.

"Yes! Yes!" I cried out loud. I pumped my fists above my head.

The evil dummy was gone. Not my problem anymore.

I didn't have to worry about sneaking him to school. I didn't have to worry about Hanson thinking I stole him.

"Yes! Yesssss!" Pure joy.

Suddenly, the pain throbbed in my nose. It was a reminder of how dangerous he could be. *He tried to take off my nose.*

He could hurt others, I realized. I was the only one who knew how to stop him.

I had no choice. I had to go after him. I crept back into the house, grabbed my coat, and headed back into the snow.

The big snowflakes were coming down hard, and the snow had started to stick on the driveway and lawn. I moved quickly down the driveway, following small shoeprints in the fresh snow. Slappy's shoeprints.

I pulled my hood down and jogged to the sidewalk. The prints of the dummy's shoes were hard to see. And the fast-falling snow was quickly covering them.

Where is he going? Where would be a natural place for him to go?

I had no idea. I took off. My sneakers slid on the icy surface. I followed the shoeprints into the street, but they disappeared in the middle of the road. I crossed and searched for them on the other side.

Slappy had passed an empty lot and was heading toward a group of small houses. Snowflakes tingled on my eyebrows. I brushed them away and tugged my hood lower.

A long, dark SUV rumbled past. The headlights rolled over me. The light made the tiny shoeprints sparkle on the snowy walk. The driver slowed, watching me. Then the big car sped away, back tires skidding on the slippery surface.

I jogged with my head lowered, squinting hard to follow the trail Slappy had left. The wind blew drifts of snow around me as I moved. And a few times I lost the trail completely and thought I would have to turn around and go home.

I stood bent over, studying the ground. My breath puffed up white steam in front of me. I found the trail again. It led up Morgan's Hill, past Morgan Park, where we go to play softball and soccer.

A patch of tall evergreen trees stood at the top of the hill. Even in the snowy, dim light, I could see that their branches were already covered in white.

I stopped to catch my breath. *Slappy, where are you taking me?*

I raised both hands and shook snow off my hood. My side began to ache from jogging uphill. I didn't remember what stood beyond the tall evergreens.

I didn't remember until I saw the low fence. And the mounds of dirt covered in snow. And the gravestones in perfect rows. The gravestones rising straight up from the snow-covered ground.

And then I realized I was at Pine Hill Cemetery. And I saw him!

Saw the dummy standing in the snow between two rows of low graves. Peering through the curtain of falling flakes, I saw Slappy watching me from the graveyard.

Watching me and beckoning with one wooden finger.

Calling me into the graveyard, that ugly grin frozen on his evil face.

17

We stood facing each other, the wind howling through the low gravestones. It took me a while to realize I was holding my breath. I let it out in a long, steamy whoosh.

Slappy rested one hand on the top of a gravestone. He beckoned to me with the other.

I didn't move. I stood like a statue, as if I'd been frozen by the cold. My brain spun. *No way* I wanted to go into the cemetery in the middle of the night. *No way* I wanted to go in there with an evil talking dummy waiting for me.

But what could I do?

Just turn and run home and climb under the covers and pretend the evil creature wasn't on the loose? It was *my fault* that Slappy was out here. And if he harmed other people . . . that would be my fault too.

I knew how to put him back to sleep. The secret words were on the sheet of paper. And I had to check his jacket pocket to see if the paper was there.

So that was the plan. Grab Slappy. Dig into his jacket pocket. Pull out the paper. Read the words out loud.

I stood there watching him, snowflakes tingling my face, the wind howling against me, as if telling me to run away.

I stood there, frozen. Trembling—not from the cold, but from my fear.

I can't. I can't go in there.

And then the dummy tossed back his head. His mouth dropped open, and he let out a chilling laugh. The laugh rang off the snow-covered trees. It seemed to bounce off the sky. The horrifying laugh surrounded me . . . a laugh so ugly, it sent chill after chill down my back—until my entire body was shaking.

And I knew I couldn't wait any longer. I had to go into the graveyard and silence Slappy so he couldn't harm anyone ever again.

I took a deep, shuddering breath. The cold air felt good in my throat. I took a step toward the gate, then another. My sneakers slid on the snowy ground. I started to stumble but grabbed the top of the gate and stopped my fall.

The metal gate squeaked as I tugged it open. I ignored my pounding heart and stepped into the cemetery. I brushed snowflakes off my eyebrows and turned to the dummy.

Slappy hadn't moved. He had stopped laughing, but that evil grin remained. His green eyes flashed with excitement. He gripped a gravestone with both hands.

My shoes crunched through a snowdrift as I made my way closer. Did he plan to run? Did he just plan to stand there? Was he about to attack?

I noticed a deep hole behind him. An empty grave. Snow covered the tall pile of dirt beside the big hole. I shivered. Was that grave waiting for a body?

"Nice night for a walk!" Slappy shouted. His raspy voice made the back of my neck tighten. "But I'm bored. It's a little *dead* out here!" He opened his mouth and laughed at his own joke.

"Slappy, what do you *want*?" I cried. My voice was muffled by the falling snow. "Why are you in this graveyard?"

"I wanted to see if you would come," he answered. His wooden lips clicked on every word. "I wanted to see if you will make a good slave. And the answer is YES! Hahahahaha!"

"I won't be your slave!" I said. My voice cracked on the word *slave*. "You can't—"

"You already *are* my slave, Owl Face!" he screamed. "I'm alive—and I'm going to stay alive! And you will be my slave . . . You will follow my every command—for the rest of your life!"

Slave to a dummy?

It almost seemed like a joke. Except he was serious.

And as I crept closer, I could actually feel the evil that surrounded him. I hesitated. What powers did he have? Did he have powers to control me, to *force* me to be his slave?

"Don't look so sad!" he cried. "I know I wasn't very nice to your nose. But . . . I had to get your attention. Hahaha! I won't hurt you again—unless you disobey me."

My eyes were on his gray sports jacket. The jacket was open, and I could see the pocket inside the lining.

Go at the count of three, I told myself. *Get that sheet of paper and read the words.*

One . . .

Two . . .

I was breathing so hard, my chest ached. I brushed snow away from my eyes. I tensed my leg muscles. Prepared to leap forward.

Three!

18

I sprang at Slappy. Raised both hands to claw at the jacket.

He uttered a startled cry. And collapsed to the snowy ground as I reached for him.

Missed. I stumbled over him. Lost my balance. Fell to my knees.

He grabbed one of my legs with both hands. He tightened his grip with surprising strength until my leg throbbed.

"Noooooo!" A moan of pain escaped my throat. I spun around—and kicked with all my might. Kicked my leg free. The dummy went toppling onto his back.

I spun around on my knees and made another grab for his jacket.

Yes!

I had the jacket tight in one hand. I reached for the pocket with my other hand.

Raw pain shot over my face as Slappy swung a hard wooden fist—*into my nose.*

He knew where to hit. He knew what would cause the most pain.

My hands dropped away from his jacket. My eyes were covered with tears as the pain radiated over my entire head. Everything went bright red. I couldn't see.

And through my pain I heard the evil dummy laughing.

"You should do something about that nose!" Slappy cried. And laughed again.

On my knees, I covered my face with both hands, hoping for the pain to fade. The dummy stood hunched, waiting for me to attack again.

I stumbled to my feet. I tried to concentrate, to think of my next move.

"Are you ready to obey, slave?" Slappy demanded.

"Good-bye," I said. "Game over. Have a nice night." I spun away from him and started to walk away. My sneakers sank into the soft snow. My face still pulsed with pain.

I walked up to the open grave. I peered down into the deep hole. Then I kept walking. I knew Slappy would follow me. He wouldn't let me get away so easily.

I was right. He came at me from behind. Tackled me, wrapping his arms around my legs.

I was ready for him. I didn't go down. I spun hard—and grabbed his waist with both hands. He let out a startled cry.

I lifted him off the ground. He began to kick both feet and thrash his fists, but I held him out at arm's length.

"Let go of me, slave!" he screamed. "I'll bury you! I'll *bury* you!"

I ignored his cries and held on to him tightly. I slid one hand to the jacket and reached inside. My fingers fumbled for the pocket.

"Let *go* of me, you owl-faced idiot!"

I grabbed the top of the pocket and slid my hand inside.

Nothing. Nothing in there.

The pocket was empty.

With a loud groan, I spun Slappy around. I grabbed the other side of the jacket. Was there a pocket in the lining on *this* side? Yes.

This had to be it.

Slappy kicked hard. His big black shoe just missed my face. A gust of wind sent a thick swirl of snow into my eyes. I could barely see. I fumbled for the other jacket pocket. Reached into it.

Nothing in there. Empty. No paper.

I slid my hands frantically up and down the jacket. No other pockets. I reached for the side of his gray trousers. No pockets in the trousers.

Failure. He didn't have the paper. I wasn't going to be able to put him back to sleep.

The dummy kicked me in the face and I loosened my grip, blinded by the red, burning pain.

My legs folded. I tried to stay up. But the next thing I knew, I was on the ground. Lying on my side. Howling in pain. I grabbed my face. Pressed my hands against my broken, throbbing nose.

"No one will ever put Slappy to sleep again!" the dummy screeched.

Then I felt his wooden hands grab my side. Before I could resist, he shoved hard. Harder than I could imagine.

Another shove. Another.

I was in too much pain to resist.

He gave a hard shove that rolled me over. And then I screamed as I started to fall. I slid down the side of the open grave.

Down . . . down in an instant. My scream following me as I hit the snowy bottom hard. I sprawled on my back. The walls of the grave rose all around me. High above my head.

Slappy's grinning face appeared over the opening of the hole. He pumped his fists over his head. "I win! Yaaaay."

"You—you can't leave me down here!" I cried. My high, shrill voice revealed my fear. "Slappy—you can't leave me here!"

"Don't bother to get up," he called down. "I know my way out. Ta-taa."

He peered down at me, the grin frozen on his face. "What's the matter, slave? Too deep to climb out? Hahaha."

I'll freeze to death down here.

No one will find me.

My terrifying thoughts paralyzed me. Blinking through the falling snow, my eyes scanned the walls. I saw that the snow had drifted to the bottom of one wall. It formed a small hill at the end of the grave. If I stood on it, I would be high enough to reach up to the top.

I glanced up. Slappy was still glaring down at me.

I took a deep breath and sprang onto the snow hill. My shoes slipped as I stumbled up. But my jump was perfect—I stretched my arms and reached the edge of the grave.

"Hey—!" Slappy cried out as I grabbed his ankle. I tightened my grip as I fell back to the grave bottom.

Squawking in surprise, he came falling down with me.

And as he came down, his big wooden head hit a rock at the top of the grave. I heard a loud *craaack*. The sound of cracking wood?

Slappy went silent. He landed on top of me. I scrambled to push him away.

I waited for him to stand up and face me. But he didn't move. His eyes were shut. His legs were tangled. His mouth hung open.

"Get up!" I shouted. "Get up!"

I grabbed him by the shoulders and shook him. "Look what you did to us!" I screamed. "Look where we are!"

I went totally berserk. I lost all control. My terror turned to anger. I kept shaking him as hard as I could. And screaming at the top of my lungs.

"We're going to freeze down here! It's all your fault. You stupid dummy! Look what you've done to us!"

Slappy didn't resist. He didn't open his eyes. Didn't try to fight me. His arms and legs bounced lifelessly as I shook him.

I tossed him to the floor of the grave. I could see a jagged line, a crack, where his head had hit the side of the grave.

I bent over him, hands gripping my waist, wheezing hard, struggling to catch my breath. Struggling to get over my panic.

The dummy remained still. The eyes stayed

shut. I gave him a soft shove with my shoe. He didn't react at all.

"Dead," I said out loud. "Slappy is dead."

Without thinking, I grabbed the dummy and placed him on top of the snow hill at the end of the grave. "Thanks for the boost, Slappy," I said. I climbed on him, reached up, grabbed the side of the grave, and pulled myself out.

With a loud groan, I picked up a huge armful of dirt and snow from the pile at the side of the open grave. And I *heaved* it down into the hole. Then I saw a shovel on the ground across from me. I grabbed it and began to shovel dirt and snow over Slappy.

Yes. I was burying him. I had to make sure that evil thing wouldn't hurt anyone else. I shoveled till my arms ached. I didn't stop until Slappy was completely covered. Buried under at least three feet of dirt.

Now I was sweating despite the cold. My dirt-smeared hands trembled. My breath came out in loud wheezes.

I hurried home. The garage door still hung wide open. I darted inside and crept into the house through the side door. No lights anywhere. The house was totally dark.

My parents are sound sleepers. They once slept through an earthquake. I was sure I could get back to my room and they'd never know I'd been out.

My shoes were leaving wet spots on the floor. I took them off and slid my feet over the spots, trying to mop them up with my socks.

I made my way slowly through the darkness to the stairs. Then I crept up the stairs one at a time, moving slowly so they wouldn't creak or squeak beneath me.

A dim light spread over the walls of the hall. My parents always keep a night-light on. Tiptoeing, I took a few steps toward my room—when Patti's door swung open and she stepped into the hall.

She gasped. "Where are *you* coming from? Did you go out?"

"Uh . . . no," I lied. "I . . . well . . . I just went downstairs for a drink of water."

She untwisted her nightshirt as she squinted at me. "In your coat? You went downstairs for a drink of water in your coat?"

I just shrugged. Then I decided to tell her the truth. "I took Slappy out," I said. "I didn't want him in the house. I got rid of him for good."

"No, you didn't," Patti said. "He's in my room right now."

20

"Huh?" I uttered a cry and staggered back against the wall. I couldn't hide my shock. "No. No way."

Patti laughed. She stuck her hand out and mussed up my hair. "You should have seen the look on your face. It was hilarious."

"You—you mean—" I stuttered.

"I mean I was joking," Patti said. "What's the big deal about that ugly dummy?"

"Nothing," I said.

My heartbeat was slowing back to normal. Her little joke had nearly given me a heart attack. "No big deal. Go back to sleep. We'll never have to think about that dummy again."

I hurried into Mr. Hanson's class ten minutes early the next morning. I wanted to catch Carlos before class started and tell him about how I buried Slappy in the graveyard. I knew Carlos would be as happy as I was that the dummy was dead and buried.

But Carlos wasn't there. We aren't supposed to use our phones in class. But since the bell hadn't rung, I took mine out and texted Carlos: Where are you? Want to talk.

I stared at the screen till he answered: Sick today. Stomach bug. Can't come to school.

I shook my head, disappointed, and tucked my phone into my backpack. When I looked up, Trevor was standing in front of my desk.

"Are you enjoying my little present?" he asked. He had a sick smile on his face. I wished I could wipe it off.

"I gave it to my sister," I lied. "She's having fun with it."

His face fell in disappointment. "You didn't bring it to life, did you?"

"No. No way," I lied some more. "I'm going to let Patti play with it for a while. Then I'm going to return it to Mr. Hanson."

Trevor turned and slumped away. I knew what he wanted to hear. He wanted to hear that Slappy came to life and terrified me and my family. He wanted to hear that he'd caused a lot of trouble for me.

No way I'd ever tell him the truth.

No way I'd ever tell Trevor he forced me to have the scariest night of my life.

The bell rang. The room grew quiet. Mr. Hanson sat on the edge of his desk and glanced around the room. He looked tired. His eyelids drooped and he had dark circles under his eyes.

94

He hadn't brushed his hair, and dark stubble shaded his face. He hadn't shaved.

"I hope everyone has recovered from the overnight," he said. "It was a disaster. I know. Sorry so many of your parents are angry at me. Believe me, I'm sorry about the whole thing."

Silence. No one spoke up. I don't think anyone knew what to say.

"The dummy hasn't been found," Hanson continued, tapping his fingers tensely on the desktop. "Perhaps he is miles from here. If I had known how evil he was . . ."

The teacher's voice trailed off. Down the row of seats, Trevor was leaning forward, staring at me.

Did he expect me to tell Hanson that I had Slappy?

Was he going to lie and say that I took the dummy?

I stared back at him, stared until he turned away.

A short while later, we were having quiet reading. I think Hanson was too exhausted to talk to us.

My desk is at the window in the back row. Maryjane Dewey sits next to me. And today she was looking at me. And smiling. She never smiles at me.

She doesn't know that I seriously crush on her. She talks to me sometimes. Almost always about schoolwork.

This morning, however, her eyes were on me.

Wait. No, not on me. She was looking at my lunch bag. Dad packs Patti and me the same lunch every morning. Some kind of boring sandwich on white bread, an apple, and a PowerBar.

Not too thrilling. So why was Maryjane eyeing it so hungrily?

She leaned closer. The room was silent, so Maryjane whispered. "Shep, what did you bring for lunch?"

"I think it's a ham and cheese sandwich," I whispered back.

She leaned closer. Her hair tickled my ear. "Can we trade?"

"Huh?"

"My mom packed tuna fish, and she knows I hate tuna fish. It's so . . . fishy."

Something moved outside the classroom window. I turned to see what it was.

"So will you trade with me?" Maryjane asked.

I gasped. Slappy!

The dummy appeared on the other side of the glass, grinning at me.

He was alive! He had escaped the grave. And he had come for me!

"We could sit at the same table in the lunch-room and share our lunches," Maryjane said. "Would you like that?"

Slappy tapped the window.

"NO!" I screamed. "NO! GO AWAY!"

21

Maryjane uttered a startled cry. "Excuse me? Shep, I thought you liked me. I—"

"Go away!" I screamed. "*Please*—go away!"

The dummy tapped his wooden forehead against the window glass.

It took me a few seconds to realize everyone in the room was staring at me. Maryjane scooted her desk away from me. Her face was an angry red.

"Shep?" Mr. Hanson set down the book he was reading and started down the aisle toward me. "Why are you screaming at Maryjane?"

"Maryjane?" I cried. "I'm not screaming at her! Don't you see him? Don't you see him out there?" I pointed frantically to the window.

Slappy had vanished.

"I . . . I don't see anything," Hanson said.

The room exploded in voices and laughter. "Shep is losing it," I heard Trevor say.

I jumped to my feet. "Didn't you hear him tap on the window?"

Hanson scratched the back of his head. "I heard that tree branch tap," he said, pointing. "It always does that if there's a breeze."

"But—but he was right outside the window!" I insisted.

Hanson put a weird smile on his face, like he was talking to a crazy person. "Shep, we're on the second floor. No one can stand outside the window."

Most everyone laughed.

I hesitated for a moment. Then I lurched toward the door. "Be right back," I said.

I heard Hanson calling after me. But I didn't stop. My shoes pounded the hall floor as I made my way downstairs to the side entrance of the building.

"Shep? Is anything wrong?" Our principal, Mrs. Hernandez, stood in her office doorway.

I didn't stop for her either.

My brain spun so hard with questions, I felt dizzy. Each question made the feeling of total terror rise in my chest.

How did Slappy get out of the open grave?

Did he come to punish me for burying him last night?

What does he plan to do to me?

I burst out of the school building, breathing hard. The snow had stopped last night. There were only two or three inches on the ground, enough to make everything look like the world was in black and white.

My breath steamed up in front of me. I glanced around.

The teachers' parking lot stood to my left. The kindergarten playground was to my right. Two women in big fur coats stood talking at the curb.

I shouted, "Slappy! Where are you? Are you here?"

The women turned toward me for a second, then returned to their conversation. A dog barked from somewhere across the street.

"I know you're here, Slappy," I shouted, cupping my hands around my mouth to form a megaphone. I shivered. It was too cold to be out here without a coat.

I took a few crunching footsteps over the snow. On the street, the two women climbed into their SUVs and drove away. I heard singing coming from a classroom behind me.

Some kids were happy and innocent. They were singing. I was out here looking for an evil dummy.

I didn't have to wait long to find him. Slappy stepped out from behind the tree at the edge of the parking lot. His red-lipped grin caught the morning sunlight. His eyes flashed excitedly.

"What do you want?" I demanded. "Why did you follow me here?"

He moved smoothly over the snow as if he were floating. I saw that his feet weren't moving at all. He *was* floating.

99

He raised an accusing hand, pointed at me. "You killed me, Shep."

"Excuse me?" I took a stumbling step back. My shoes almost slid out from under me in the snow. "How did you get out?" I cried. "What do you want? What are you doing here?"

"You killed me," he repeated. His wooden lips clicked with each word.

He floated closer.

"I did not!" I shouted. "You know it was an accident. You fell and hit your head. It was an accident."

"*You're* about to have a very bad accident, Shep," Slappy rasped.

"No—!" I cried. "I'm taking you back to Hanson. He'll find a way to put you back to sleep."

That made him toss back his head and laugh. His ugly cackle rang off the trees and the snowy ground.

I didn't hesitate. I took a deep breath. And dove for him.

I reached my arms out wide to capture him.

Sliding on the snow, I dove forward. Made a grab. *And my hands went RIGHT THROUGH him!*

22

He floated back, hands raised above his head.

I made another grab. Again, my hands slid right through him, as if he were made of air.

He laughed again. "Hey, Shep—what does it feel like to be an idiot? Asking for a friend. Hahahaha!"

"You—you're a *ghost*!" I finally caught on.

"Good boy. And what do ghosts do?"

"Huh?"

"What do ghosts do, Owl Face?"

I suddenly pictured Annalee. Coming for me, that dangerous look on her face. Reaching for me . . .

"They . . . haunt people," I said.

Slappy floated up until he was three or four feet in the air. He hovered over me, his eyes now spinning wildly. "You killed me, Shep," he repeated. "Now I have no choice. I'm a ghost and I'm going to haunt you—*forever*."

"No—listen," I pleaded. "I'm sorry. I—"

"Don't be sorry, Shep. Be happy that you've

101

made a friend for life! Just think—I'll always be there!" He laughed again. The cold, raspy laughter sent a shudder down my whole body.

I heard the crunch of footsteps behind me. I turned back to see Mr. Hanson and Mrs. Hernandez hurrying toward me.

"Shep, what are you doing out here?" Hanson called.

I spun around.

Slappy's ghost had vanished.

"I . . . uh . . . thought I saw something," I stammered.

"Are you okay? Why are you out here in the cold?" Mrs. Hernandez demanded. She took my arm. "Come inside, Shep. Do you want to see the nurse?"

"Shep had a strange outburst in class," Hanson told her as we made our way back into the school. "He screamed at Maryjane Dewey, who sits next to him. He screamed for her to go away."

"No. That's not true," I said. "It . . . it's a long story."

"Should I call your parents?" Mrs. Hernandez asked.

I shivered. The warmth of the school building settled over me. I glanced all around. Did Slappy's ghost follow me inside?

No sign of him.

"I'm okay now," I said. "Really. I just needed some fresh air. I'm perfectly fine."

They both eyed me suspiciously. Finally, the principal said, "Okay, Shep. Get back to class."

Of course, there was no way I could relax in class. Or pay attention. All of my attention was on the window beside me. I kept expecting the Slappy ghost to reappear at any time, to grin at me and tease me. To haunt me.

But he didn't show up. Lunchtime came, and I was very happy to get away from that window. As I carried my lunch bag to the lunchroom, I thought about Carlos. I hoped he wasn't too sick. I needed him. I needed him to help me think of a way to get rid of Slappy's ghost.

I saw Maryjane Dewey at a table in the back. She was surrounded by Courtney Levitt and Dawn Meadows and some of her other friends. I think she was deliberately not looking at me.

I decided to go over to her table and apologize. I knew I'd ruined my chance to be her friend. I'd shouted at her and told her to go away. At least, that's what she thought.

I stepped up to her table. Maryjane pretended to be interested in what was in her lunch bag.

Courtney had a big bowl of spaghetti in front of her. Dawn was starting to fork up a big slice of custard pie.

I suddenly lost my nerve. I wanted to apologize to Maryjane. But all the words had left my head.

They were staring at me in silence, waiting for me to say something.

103

"I . . . uh . . . How's the spaghetti?" I said to Courtney.

"Not bad," she said. And then the spaghetti bowl raised up. It lifted off the table. It floated up by itself—and flew onto my head.

Oh, wow. The bowl smashed over my hair, and I was blinded for a few seconds as the spaghetti oozed down over my face.

The spaghetti rolled onto my shirt. Piles of it clung to my shoulders.

Maryjane and her friends were all gasping in shock. "Courtney—did you throw your spaghetti on him?" Maryjane demanded.

"No. No way!" Courtney cried. "I didn't touch it!"

I spit out some noodles. "I guess it just slipped off the table onto my head," I said sarcastically.

That made the girls start to laugh.

"It isn't funny!" I cried. "I—I—"

That's when the plate in front of Dawn shot up into the air. It flew at me, too fast to duck. And the custard pie smacked my face. The plate clattered to the floor. The pie covered my eyes, my nose. I struggled to breathe.

"I didn't do it!" Dawn screamed. "I swear!"

I wiped pie off my face with both hands. I knew who was doing this. Slappy. Slappy was using me for his own private food fight.

And as I wiped away spaghetti and custard pie, I heard the laughter. The girls were laughing.

Everyone was laughing. Even the teachers were all laughing at the teachers' table.

No one was laughing more than Maryjane. She actually had tears running down her cheeks.

And over the laughter, I could hear Slappy's raspy cackle. He was haunting me. Ruining my life. And he would haunt me until . . . until . . . forever.

23

I texted Carlos on my way home. He said he was feeling better and he would come over. I hoped he would have some ideas about how to deal with Slappy. He was the only person I could count on.

I walked into the house from the back door. I kicked off my snowy shoes and dropped my backpack onto the kitchen counter. Then I started to unzip my coat.

"Anyone home?" I shouted.

No answer. This was strange, since my parents both worked at home. I grabbed a can of Coke from the fridge and headed toward the front of the house. "Mom? Dad? Are you here?"

I heard a rustling sound, soft, like someone crinkling paper. And then a scrape.

"Hey—who's home?" I shouted. "Patti? Are you here? Who—?"

I stopped when I saw the dim glow of light from the end of the hall. A flickering circle of yellow light. It grew brighter as it expanded. As I stared, the light filled the hall, so bright now I shielded my eyes.

And I recognized the dark form inside. Annalee!

Annalee floated out from the light, her pale face stern, angry, her eyes locked on mine.

"N-no!" I stammered.

Now I was being haunted by *two* ghosts. And both of them wanted to hurt me.

Annalee's coppery hair flew behind her as she came toward me. She didn't blink. Her eyes stared as if trying to burn into my brain.

Two ghosts . . . Two ghosts . . .

"This isn't fair!" I yelled.

No one else was home. I huddled there, alone, with the ghost moving slowly toward me. She raised one hand and pointed. Her pale lips moved, but no sound came out.

Was she saying my name?

I staggered back. I concentrated on her hand. She kept curling her fingers, reaching for me.

And suddenly, my fright turned to anger. *This isn't fair.* I took a deep breath and screamed at her, screamed at the top of my lungs. And shook both fists above my head.

"Stop! Leave me ALONE! Go away! I mean it! GO AWAY!"

To my shock, she stopped. The light appeared to dim behind her. She lowered her hand. And her hard expression faded. She turned her eyes to the floor.

And vanished in a puff of cold air.

The cold air brushed over me. I blinked a few times. Did my shout really chase her away? Was she gone for good?

A loud crash behind me answered my question. Annalee was back!

No!

I swallowed hard, fighting back my fear. It wasn't a crash. It was a knock on the back door. My legs were unsteady as I lurched into the kitchen to let Carlos in.

"Are you sick?" I asked.

He shrugged. "A stomach thing. My parents think I ate too much candy last night. It's hard to stop after only one Snickers bar, you know?"

I handed him a Coke and we went up to my room to talk. We both sat on the floor, our backs against my bed.

I told him all about last night. About the graveyard. About how Slappy hit his head. How I buried him. And how his ghost came to haunt me in school today.

He kept sipping his Coke as he listened. He didn't interrupt or say anything. I couldn't tell whether he believed it or not.

Finally, he said, "Where is that piece of paper? You know, the one with the words on it? The words your sister read out loud?"

I sighed. "I don't know, Carlos. I've searched everywhere. I tore up my room and Patti's room looking for it. And I searched the dummy's pockets. It just disappeared into thin air."

We both sat staring at the carpet.

"How do I get rid of him? We need an idea."

We stared at the carpet some more.

Carlos grabbed his stomach. "Whoa. I'm feeling a little weird again. I'd better get home. Don't want to be sick for my party."

He set the Coke can down, climbed to his feet, and started toward the door. I followed him down the stairs.

"If you have any ideas . . ." I said. "I'm kind of stumped."

"Let's talk about it after my party," Carlos said. He stopped at the front door. "Shep, you could Google 'ghosts.' There might be some tips there."

Then he hurried away. He was no help at all.

I climbed back up to my room and did another search for the piece of paper with the words on it. Again, no luck.

I couldn't relax. I couldn't feel like myself. Every sound made me jump. Every flash of light, every shadow made me think that one of the ghosts was back.

At dinner, Patti asked me where the dummy was. She said she wanted to play with it.

"I returned it to Mr. Hanson," I lied. If only.

I tried to keep calm. It wasn't easy. I know there are laws against strangling your sister. But in this case, she kind of deserved it. I mean, she had put me in terrible danger.

And late that night, the danger turned terrifying.

I was just drifting off to sleep. I'd tried for hours, turning onto my side, then my back. But I was too tense to sleep.

And then when I finally started to fade, I heard a tapping at my bedroom window. I sat up, instantly alert. A chill tightened my neck.

I gazed at the window. It was open because I like it to be cold in my room when I sleep. In the light from the streetlamp at the curb, I saw something floating in the window.

It took my eyes a few seconds to focus.

Slappy's head!

Just his grinning head bobbing in the window, staring in at me.

"NOOOOO!" I let out a cry and leaped out of bed. My feet tangled in the bedsheet and I fell to my knees.

Slappy's laughter rang out through the room. I scrambled to my feet. The head floated in the window, bobbing up and down like a balloon. The rest of him was invisible.

I had to make him stop. I wasn't thinking clearly. I was still half asleep. I tugged my feet from the tangled bedsheet—and hurtled myself to the window.

In the dim light from below, the head bobbed in front of me. Slappy rolled his eyes and uttered his ugly cackle.

I shot forward. Stuck out my hands. Grabbed at the laughing dummy head.

The head darted backward.

My hands slipped through it.

I couldn't stop myself in time. I didn't have time to scream.

The cold night seemed to swallow me as I fell headfirst out the window.

25

"Owww." I landed hard on my shoulder on the shingle roof that slants down from my bedroom window.

I grabbed for the windowsill, but it was already out of my reach.

I began to roll down the roof, my body bumping the cold shingles as I came down. I grabbed frantically at the shingles. Grabbed at *anything*.

But I couldn't stop my fall.

I'm going to die.

I'm so high off the ground. I'm going to die.

As I spun down, I saw the grinning dummy head floating above me. Watching. Enjoying my doom.

"Join me! Join me!" Slappy screeched. "We can be ghosts together!"

"Noooo!" I protested. I rolled to the end of the roof. I started to slip off the side.

With a loud groan, I made a desperate grab with both hands. I grabbed the cold metal gutter at the bottom of the slanting roof. Grabbed it with both hands and held on. Held on . . .

My feet dangling below me in midair. The gutter cutting into my hands. I gripped the gutter . . . held on . . . held on . . .

Behind me, I heard Slappy's laughter. "Hang on!" he screamed. "Hang on! You don't want to go *splaaat*—do you?" He laughed some more, enjoying his triumph.

My arms began to ache. The metal cut into my skin. My body hung heavily down the side of the house. I couldn't hold on for long. I was about to become a ghost like Slappy.

With one last burst of energy, I swung my body to one side. Holding on tightly, I swung myself to the other side. Again. And then I swung my leg up . . . swung my foot onto the shingle roof.

Yes!

Still gripping the gutter, I swung my entire leg onto the roof. Then I gave a hard push. Was I strong enough?

"Whoa!" I cried out as I managed to swing my other leg onto the roof.

I did it. I was lying on the shingles. Slowly, carefully, I used my hands to claw my way up the roof. Breathing so hard I thought my chest would burst. Slowly . . . slowly . . .

Slappy's laughter faded as I grabbed the bedroom windowsill with both hands. I tightened my grip and pulled myself into my bedroom.

"Ohhhhh." With a long moan, I dropped to the carpet. I lay there for a long while, struggling to catch my breath, to slow my heartbeats.

When I finally stood up, Slappy's ghost was gone.

I survived tonight. But what about tomorrow?

26

Carlos had a beautiful day for his birthday party. The sun was bright and high in a clear blue sky. Most of the snow on the ground had melted away.

I was a little late getting to the stable because Dad had to do some errands before he dropped me off. When we drove through the stable gates, I saw that some kids were gathered around the food table and some kids were already on horseback, riding on the trails that led to the woods. Carlos had invited the entire class. Even Trevor. "If Trevor gives us any trouble, we'll make him clean up after the horses!" Carlos said.

"Have fun. Try to stay on your horse," Dad said as I opened the car door.

"Thanks for the encouragement, Dad," I said sarcastically. He knew I was nervous about my first horseback ride. Sometimes he has a sick sense of humor.

Carlos was standing with his parents near the

stable office at the far end. Behind them, I saw a pile of wrapped birthday presents. Gripping my present for him, I started toward them.

Music poured from a tall black speaker nearby. Carlos's dad is a DJ on weekends at parties and weddings. He had set up his DJ equipment behind the speaker. The horse stalls were decorated with red and blue balloons. They bobbed in the soft breeze.

Some kids were already returning from their horseback rides. The horses walked slowly. A trainer from the stable walked along beside each horse. A short line had formed of kids waiting their turn.

I turned my gaze and suddenly realized I was walking beside Maryjane Dewey. She had pretty much ignored me since the screaming incident in class. And since Slappy covered me in spaghetti and pie in the lunchroom.

"Awesome day for a party," I said.

She nodded. "Feels like spring."

I glanced at the present she was carrying. "What did you get Carlos?" I asked.

"A game," she said. "*Space Panthers*."

"Hey, so did I!" I cried.

She stopped walking and narrowed her eyes at me. "You bought him the same game I did?"

I nodded, grinning.

"You creep!" She stomped away, taking long, angry strides.

Hey, it's not my fault, I thought. I watched her say hi to Carlos and his parents. Then she tossed her present onto the pile. I guessed she planned to be angry at me for the rest of my life.

Carlos and I low-fived each other and bumped knuckles. "Awesome party," I told his parents. Mr. Jackson went to change the music. Carlos's mom began talking to the guy who was piling up charcoal at the grill.

"I can't hang out right now," Carlos said. "My mom says I have to be polite and greet people."

"No problem," I said. I spotted Trevor in the line for horseback rides. He saw me too. He flashed me two thumbs-down.

Funny guy.

"Go take your horseback ride before the line gets too long," Carlos said. "When you get back, we can hang out."

I nodded okay, turned, and started toward the line of kids. I stopped when I glimpsed the birthday cake on the food table. It was so tall, like a tower of chocolate icing.

"Wow. That cake looks excellent," I said.

"My aunt Maria is a baker," Carlos replied. "She's wild. The cake is almost as tall as I am!"

I trotted up to the line. I wasn't happy to be right behind Trevor, but I had no choice. He turned to me as a trainer brought Trevor's horse up beside him.

"Whatever you do, Shep," Trevor said, "don't ride the horse named Lightning."

"Huh? Lightning?"

Trevor nodded. "Yeah. It's a real high-strung horse. Needs an expert rider. Stay away from her. That's what they told me."

The trainer was an older guy with a grizzle of white beard over his face and a yellow baseball cap pulled down over his forehead. He wore a red-and-black flannel shirt over tight, faded jeans.

He set a stool down for Trevor and gave him a boost onto his horse. "Have you ever ridden before?" he asked.

Trevor nodded. "Yeah. I've had some lessons." Trevor patted the back of the horse's head. "What's this horse's name?"

"Buttermilk," the trainer answered. He grabbed the bridle and began to lead the horse to the path.

I took a deep breath. The air smelled of burning charcoal. The fire for lunch had been started. A few more kids joined the line behind me.

I saw a young woman walking a horse toward the line. The horse was pure white and very tall. It made a prancing move with its front legs as the woman led it forward.

She stopped beside me. The horse tossed its head and made a soft whinnying sound. "Your turn," the woman said. "What's your name?"

"Shep."

"Mine is Greta." She placed the footstool beside the horse. "Let me help you up."

I slid onto the saddle and fumbled around a bit, getting my shoes into the stirrups.

"Don't look so scared. This is going to be fun," Greta said. "Have you ridden before?"

"First time," I said. I glanced down. I was so far from the ground!

"Just hold on tight to the saddle horn here, and you'll be fine." She moved my hands to the leather horn that rose up in the front of the saddle.

"Ready?" she asked.

"Sure. Ready," I said. "What's this horse's name?"

"Lightning," she said.

27

She started to lead Lightning to the path. I gripped the saddle horn tightly with both hands. The horse kept her head down as we slowly moved.

"Uh . . . do you have another horse?" I asked.

"You'll like Lightning," Greta said. "She's very responsive. We'll just walk. You don't have to trot. When you feel more comfortable, you can let go of the horn and take the reins."

"Yeah. When I'm more comfortable," I said.

The horse seemed to bounce as she walked. She kind of swayed from side to side, and I kept feeling as if I'd slide off.

The path led up the hill of the pasture, which was still pretty much covered in snow. A woods of snow-covered trees stood at the top.

Holding on to the reins, Greta walked beside me, keeping perfect pace with the horse. "Are you starting to feel more comfortable?" she asked.

"Not yet," I said. My hands were aching from gripping the saddle horn so tightly.

"We can turn around anytime, if you're not enjoying it," she said.

I opened my mouth to reply—but stopped when I saw the figure float up in front of us.

Slappy.

Slappy's ghost was a few feet away, hovering high off the ground, above the horse's head.

"Noooo!" My shout startled Greta. She dropped the reins. "What is it?" she cried.

"Don't you see him?" I shouted.

She shook her head. "See *what*?"

Slappy tilted back his head and laughed his rattling cackle.

Lightning lurched. She raised her head.

The horse saw Slappy!

Still cackling, Slappy floated closer. The horse let out a loud, whinnying protest—and rose up onto her back legs.

I started to slide off. I uttered a cry and grasped the saddle horn.

I saw the confused look on Greta's face. She made a frantic grab for the reins.

Missed.

The horse whinnied again. She bucked her head up and down, then took off, galloping into the trees. Off the path. Into the woods.

Oh, help me. This isn't happening.

I bounced on her broad back. My legs flew out

from the horse's sides. I gripped the saddle horn with one hand and reached under my shirt for my lucky silver bear charm with the other.

It was gone!

In my panic, I remembered I'd taken it off in my bath last night.

Slappy's ghost stayed ahead of us. He floated just above our heads, his hands flapping out at his sides, his mouth open in a never-ending laugh.

Low tree limbs brushed the top of my head as Lightning galloped farther into the woods, running crazily, zigzagging, whinnying in terror the whole way. I ducked my head as low as I could and held on.

I could hear Greta's cries for help far behind me.

Pounding hooves. I felt every *thud* the hooves made against the hard ground. I bounced hard in the saddle. Staring at the flying ghost of Slappy ahead of us.

And then the horse wheeled around. Raised her front legs high and spun back toward the pasture.

I screamed again as we went galloping full-speed toward the stable. I leaned forward. Wrapped my arms around the horse's neck. Practically strangled her as we galloped. Shut my eyes. Shut my eyes and listened to the heavy *thud* of the hoofbeats.

I opened my eyes when I heard screams. The other horses skittered wildly as Lightning charged at them. Some kids fell to the ground in fear. Others ran to get out of my way as Lightning flew to the stable.

The air was filled with their shrieks.

"Stop, Lightning! Stop!" I cried out.

Holding on to her neck, I struggled to slow her down. But I couldn't manage it. Slappy had terrified her beyond control.

The big horse ran headlong into the food table. I saw Carlos's mother hit the ground to get out of the way.

Food flew in all directions. The tall chocolate cake rose up in the air—flipped over—and came down on top of a boy. Trevor! The cake landed on Trevor's head, covered him, appeared to *swallow* him!

And then Lightning kicked over the charcoal grill. Hot coals flew into the air. Kids screamed as they struggled to get out of the way.

Lightning reared up and knocked over the DJ equipment. The speaker toppled to the ground.

"You ruined my party! You ruined my party!" I heard Carlos shriek.

No time to think about it. The horse slammed into one of the stalls at the back of the stable. Kicked high. And I went sailing to the ground.

I landed hard on my back. My breath whooshed out. Pain rolled over me.

My first horseback ride was over. And suddenly, I knew what I had to do.

28

The birthday party broke up early. Everything was destroyed. There was no reason for anyone to stay.

Carlos wouldn't even let me explain. When I started to tell him it was Slappy's ghost that caused the trouble, he just scowled at me. "Maybe Slappy's ghost can be your best friend now," he said. He stomped away.

The ghost was ruining my life. Actually, he was trying to *end* my life. I had to find a way to defeat him. But how do you defeat a ghost?

You can't.

And that's what led me to my desperate plan. My plan to dig the Slappy dummy up from the graveyard and bring him back to life. *Then* try to get rid of him.

What was I thinking? I was thinking it would be easier to deal with a *dummy* than with a *ghost*.

Even if I couldn't find the words to put Slappy to sleep, I could lock him in a closet. Or shut him up in a suitcase in the basement. A living Slappy wouldn't be able to *haunt* me.

That's what I thought about as Dad drove me home from the party in silence. "We'll probably have to pay the Jacksons for the damage you did" was the only thing Dad said, when we were nearly home.

I muttered a reply. I was too busy going over and over my plan in my head. *No way* I wanted to go back to that graveyard. But I knew if I didn't, Slappy's ghost would ruin more than a birthday party. He'd ruin my whole life.

And so, that evening, when Mom and Dad went into town to go shopping with Patti, I gathered my courage and walked back to the cemetery.

It was a warm, clear night. But that didn't keep me from shivering the whole way. I pulled up my hood and zipped my coat right to my chin as I approached the cemetery. Silvery moonlight washed over the rows of graves. There were still patches of snow all around.

I pushed through the creaking gate and stepped up to the first row of gravestones. Where was it? Where was the hole where I had buried Slappy? It had been so dark that night, and I had been so afraid.

I began to walk back and forth, moving from row to row. Finally, I found the spot halfway back and on the far side. The grave was only half filled in. The shovel was still where I left it.

I jumped into the hole and began to scoop up dirt and toss it out. The snow had melted and the dirt was wet and muddy.

I worked feverishly, frantically digging the shovel in, heaving the dirt up to the graveside. Sweat rolled down my forehead. My arms throbbed with pain. Again. Again. Dig and toss.

Finally, I hit something. I bent to examine it. One of the dummy's arms.

I lowered both hands into the dirt. And began to shove the dirt away, pawing it like an animal.

I was gasping for breath by the time I was able to reach down and lift the dummy from the grave. I shook it hard, forcing clumps of dirt to fall off.

"I'll clean you up when we get home," I said, my voice hoarse and weak from my hard work.

I raised the lifeless dummy to the ground. Climbed out of the hole. Brushed dirt off the front of my coat. Lifted Slappy. Flung him over my shoulder. And carried him home.

My family was still out shopping. I didn't want them to see me with the dummy. I carried it down to the basement and turned on all the lights. I set it down on my dad's worktable and raised the head into the light so I could see it clearly.

The back of Slappy's head had a jagged cut. The cut was very narrow. Not wide at all.

Could I bring the dummy back to life by repairing the cut? Filling in the crack? Maybe Krazy Glue would do the job?

I had no way of knowing whether Krazy Glue would repair Slappy and bring him back. No clue. But it was my *only* idea.

I pulled open the worktable drawer and fumbled through all the bottles and tubes and tools, screws and nails. My fingers wrapped around a tube of the glue.

My hand trembled as I opened the cap. I held the dummy's head firmly in one hand. And tilted the glue into the crack. I squeezed the tube until it was almost empty.

The glue filled in the crack. A little glue ran down the back of his head to his neck. I waited for the glue to dry. Then I sat the dummy up on the worktable.

"Please come to life," I told it. "Please come back to life."

I stood there staring at the lifeless thing. Its arms hung limply at its sides. The eyes were closed. It didn't move.

"Please . . . Please. You're back together now. Please come back to life."

I gasped as the dummy opened its eyes. The wide, grinning mouth moved up and down. Slappy slowly raised both hands. And wrapped them around my throat.

"Let go!" I cried.

The wooden fingers tightened their grip. The dummy's eyes flashed with excitement. *"I'm back, slave!"* he rasped.

With a hard tug, I struggled to free myself from his grasp. But he was too strong. "Can't . . . breathe . . ." I choked out.

A stirring behind me made me stop struggling.

I wasn't alone. "Mom? Dad? Patti? Are you back?"

A pulsing white light made me spin around. And I stared at Annalee rising up behind me. Her hair fluttered behind her shoulders. Her eyes were cold blue, cold as ice.

"Help me!" I gasped. "Annalee—please! Help me!"

She floated closer. She raised a pale hand, and I saw a sheet of paper gripped tightly in it.

"Annalee—"

She narrowed her icy eyes at me. "These are the words," she whispered, her voice light as air. "These are the words to put the dummy back to sleep—forever."

Slappy let go of my throat. He stabbed his hand forward. *"Give me that paper!"* he barked at Annalee.

She swung it away from him. Her eyes were locked on me. "Shep, you always ran from me. You never stayed to talk to me, to learn my story."

"I . . . I . . ." I didn't know what to say. My eyes were on the paper she waved in her hand.

"Don't you know why I had to haunt your house?" Annalee cried. "Don't you know why ghosts linger on the earth?"

"N-no," I stammered. "No. Why?"

"Ghosts linger because they have unfinished business," Annalee said. "I can't leave till I do a good deed." She lowered her head. "I led a very selfish life. I owe one good deed. One good deed and I can go happily to the beyond."

"Yes. Please!" I cried. "Do your one good deed now. Rescue me, Annalee. Read the words. Put this evil dummy to sleep."

I pointed to the paper in her hand. "Please. Read the words. I'm sorry I never listened to you. I'm sorry I always ran away from you. But, please—do your one good deed now. This is your chance."

A smile crossed her pale face. "Yes. Yes, I will do it now," she said. "One last good deed."

She raised the slip of paper in front of her.

And ripped it into tiny pieces.

30

I watched in horror as the tiny shreds of paper scattered on the basement floor. "But—but—" I sputtered.

"I did my good deed," Annalee told me. "Not for you, Shep. For Slappy!"

"But—but—"

"Slappy never ignored me. He never screamed at me to go away." The white light began to pulse behind her. "And now that I've done my final good deed on earth . . . good-bye to you."

The light appeared to swallow her. It flashed brightly, so bright I had to cover my eyes. And when I uncovered them, Annalee was gone.

Still blinking, I turned to Slappy, sitting on the worktable, swinging his legs, his grin wide. "Nice girl," he rasped. "Sorry I didn't get a chance to know her better."

He leaned forward, his big, glassy eyes on me. "Now, slave . . . where *were* we? Hahahahahaha."

EPILOGUE FROM SLAPPY

Hahahahaha!

I LOVE a story with a happy ending—don't you?

Maybe it wasn't a happy ending for Shep, my awesome new slave. But I thought Annalee showed a lot of good taste. Smart girl.

Maybe *I'll* do a good deed someday.

Hahaha. Just kidding.

Why do a good deed when it's so much more fun to be scary and evil?

Speaking of *scary*, I'll be back before you know it with another Goosebumps story.

Remember, this is *SlappyWorld*.

You only *scream* in it!

IT'S ALIVE! IT'S ALIVE!

Here's a sneak peek!

1

"I dreamed our robot came alive and went ber-serk," I told Jayden. We were walking home from school, and, of course, we were talking about robotics. Because we are obsessed.

A yellow school bus rolled by, and some kids shouted at us from the windows. I waved at them, but I didn't bother to see who they were. I was busy telling Jayden about my dream.

My name is Livvy Jones. I'm twelve, and I have very real, very exciting dreams, and in the morning, I remember every single one of them. I think it's good to tell people your dreams because they can help you figure out what they mean.

So I told Jayden my dream. "The robot ran away, and I chased after it. But it was too fast for me. It ran to a big parking lot and it began picking up cars. It lifted them high in the air, then smashed them to the pavement."

Jayden had a thoughtful look on his face. Of course, he always has a thoughtful look on his face. That's Jayden's thing. He's quiet and he's thoughtful. His dark eyes gazed straight ahead, and he kept nodding his head thoughtfully as he listened to me.

"The robot smashed one car after another. It was a very noisy dream," I said. "I think all the crashing and smashing is what woke me up. I sat straight up in bed and I was shaking. The dream was so real."

We crossed the street. Jayden continued to look thoughtful.

"So? What do you think it means?" I said.

He scratched his head. He has curly black hair that pops straight up. He can't keep it down. It's like it's alive, some kind of sponge life.

We turned and cut through the Murphys' backyard. They probably wouldn't like our shortcut through their yard every afternoon, but they're never home. My house is three doors down.

"I think it means that we shouldn't have made our robot look so human," Jayden said finally.

"Huh? What do you mean?"

"Everyone else is building robots that look like machines," he continued. "But we built ours to look like a girl. And I think maybe that's what is freaking you out. We built a girl. It's too real."

"But I love Francine," I said.

Jayden rolled his eyes. "We can't call a robot Francine. No way."

"Why not?"

"Because you can't. You just can't have a robot named Francine."

I gave him a playful shove. "She is my idea and I get to name her."

"No way, Livvy," Jayden whined. "Francine. Francine the Robot. It's too . . . embarrassing." He crossed his arms in front of his chest. "I'm going to talk to Harrison about it. Seriously."

Harrison Teague is the coach of our robotics team. He is a good guy. And he keeps us psyched. He's keeping us pumped up and eager to beat Swanson Academy in the Springdale Robotics Meet this year. Swanson Academy is where all the rich kids go. They're our rival, our enemy school. In football, in basketball—in *everything*.

Harrison doesn't know that much about robotics. He admits it himself. I mean, he's the girls' basketball coach, and the school gave him the robotics team to coach in his spare time. They sort of forced it on him.

I stopped outside my family's garage. I lowered my backpack to the driveway. "Listen, Jayden, we can't argue about the robot's name now. We are so close to finishing her. We just have a few tweaks to make on the programming. This is no time to fight."

He shrugged. "You're right. I think she's ready for us to test some of her skills this afternoon." He pumped a fist above his head. "This is exciting, Livvy."

It *was* exciting. Jayden and I had been building the robot in my garage for months. Programming her computer brain took weeks and weeks.

And now we were finally about to see what she could do.

My family has a white-shingled, two-car garage. But my parents never put their cars in the garage. They always park them in the driveway. That gave Jayden and me the perfect workshop to build Francine.

I bent down and grabbed the door on the left. Jayden helped me, and we both pushed the door up.

"Let's see what we have here," Jayden said, rubbing his hands together like a mad scientist in a horror movie. "How is our little experiment?"

We both stopped. We both stared. We both uttered startled cries.

"The robot . . ." I murmured. "She's GONE!"

What was the first thing I thought of?

My dream, of course.

Once again, I saw the robot running down the street. Picking up cars. Smashing them on the pavement.

Is that what happened here? Did my dream come true? Did Francine run away?

Of course not. She wasn't programmed to walk very far. And she definitely wasn't programmed to open the garage door and then close it again.

Jayden and I stood in the center of the garage, staring at the spot where the robot should have been.

"Have we been robbed?" Jayden said finally. His voice came out tiny and a little bit shaky.

I opened my mouth to reply but stopped when I heard laughter.

"Whoa!" I spun around to the open door.

Jayden sighed. "I recognize that laugh."

So did I.

We both dove out of the garage—and saw Chaz Fremont on the patio. He stood there laughing his hee-haw donkey laugh with one arm around Francine.

Yes. He had Francine.

He had been hiding behind the garage, waiting for us. Waiting to give Jayden and me a little scare. Because Chaz loves to torture us and torment us and tease us and bully us and give us a hard time.

He's not our favorite dude.

Also, I have to mention this—Chaz doesn't go to Springdale Middle School like Jayden and me. He goes to Swanson Academy.

And I have to tell you one more thing about Chaz, who has short spiky red hair and freckles on his big round face, and tiny blue eyes that look like bird eyes, and is big and hulky and works out a lot. He's the captain of the Swanson Academy Robotics Team, which beats us at the meet every year. Because Chaz is a *genius* robot builder.

I don't like him, but I have to say that to be fair.

"What are you doing with Francine?" I demanded.

Chaz's mouth dropped open. "Francine? You can't call a robot Francine. I think you should call it Livvy-II because it looks just like you, except a lot cuter. Haha."

"You're not funny," I said. "Give us back our robot."

"Sure. You can have it." He slid his arm off Francine's shoulders and took a few steps back. "I was just pulling your chain. I forgot you don't have a sense of humor."

"You're about as funny as pig vomit," Jayden said.

"Oh, good one," Chaz replied. "Did you just make that up?"

Jayden blushed. He blushes easily, and Chaz always knows how to make him blush.

Jayden and I lifted our robot off the patio stones and began carrying her into the garage. She weighed a ton. We had used molded sheet metal for the body. And the computer that held all the brain modules was also heavy.

Chaz followed us, cracking his knuckles in front of him as he walked, one of his gross habits. "What does it do?" he asked. "Wave bye-bye? Or was that too hard for you to program?"

"Why would we tell you?" I shot back. "You're the enemy, remember?"

"I'm the frenemy," Chaz said. "Remember? Robotics is all about *cooperatition*."

That's a word some robotics coach made up somewhere. A combination of *cooperation* and *competition*. It means we cooperate and compete at the same time. "Robotics is the most friendly competition." That's what Harrison Teague keeps reminding us all the time.

Chaz picked up a pair of hedge clippers from a shelf and pretended to cut Francine's head off.

About the Author

R.L. Stine's books are read all over the world. So far, his books have sold more than 300 million copies, making him one of the most popular children's authors in history. Besides Goosebumps, R.L. Stine has written the teen series Fear Street and the funny series Rotten School, as well as the Mostly Ghostly series, The Nightmare Room series, and the two-book thriller *Dangerous Girls*. R.L. Stine lives in New York with his wife, Jane, and Minnie, his King Charles spaniel. You can learn more about him at RLStine.com.

The Original Bone-Chilling Series